THE SHERIFF
OF SINGING RIVER

1.

A bad situation was getting worse—or better—according to the way one looked at it. It had been raining since dawn, when Boone Sarsfield had left the train and boarded the stage; a cold, soaking rain, presaging the end of summer and the beginning of fall, whipped by a gusty wind. A normally rough and unpleasant ride had been rendered approximately twice as uncomfortable as usual.

Old Felix Yankus, who was a careful driver when sober, had taken several nips from proffered flasks at the change-houses along the way, to warm himself against the raw chill. Now, as these potations took effect, he was driving with increasing recklessness, sending the six horses ahead at a headlong pace. The rapidly falling dark and partially washed-out road had lost their power to impress him.

Inside the coach, it was dryer but no less dark, and the passage was even rougher. A wild lurch threw his adjoining seatmate into Boone's arms, for perhaps the twentieth time during the ride. For a time she had sought to restrain herself, but, finding that it was easier to sway with the motion, had given up trying to fight the inevitable. For an instant, aware that red lips were close to his own, Boone was tempted to take advantage of the darkness and kiss them, but restrained the impulse.

Disentangling herself again, Miss Hankinson commented somewhat wryly. He could see that her perky little bonnet was jammed over one eye, black as the hair above, which could still sparkle with mischievous humor at the end of so long a day.

"I'm done apologizin', Mr. Sarsfield, though you'll think I'm a forward creature, throwin' myself at you this way!" she gasped. "But you just do seem to attract me!"

"Why, now, ma'am that's about the nicest thing I ever had said to me," Boone assured her. "It's a real pleasure to serve as a buffer for so charmin' a lady." Next time, he feared, he might not be able to refrain.

The Hankinsons, brother and sister, had boarded the stage along with him. During the day he had learned, with a quickening expectancy, that their destination was the same as his own, Singing River. Only they were newcomers, fresh out of the East, while he was heading homeward to the Moon Star Ranch, after a trip to Chicago.

He'd been tempted to ask what brought them to

such a place, but had figured it would be better not to overplay his luck. Helen Hankinson he judged to be about twenty, her brother Bob a year or so her junior. Bob was quieter and equally cheerful, despite the discomforts. Already they were like old friends, Helen particularly. Something about her gave Boone a sense of having seen or known her somewhere before, although that was manifestly impossible.

Five other passengers jammed the coach past the point of even reasonable comfort, preferring that to the buffeting of the elements. Four of them Boone found less than noteworthy, but he had paid attention to the man who had given his name as Peabody—partly because Peabody had watched him so sharply, the rest of the time favoring Helen Hankinson with a similar regard. His watchfulness reminded Boone of a cat lying in wait for a mouse.

Still, there was something about the man, from the long, thin cigars which he smoked to the rusty trousers tucked into down-at-heel boots, a quality which suggested charm and dash—even if it too was somewhat frayed.

"You're just back from a trip to Chicago, Mr. Sarsfield?" Peabody asked now, while the rain lashed the doors and swirled in mistily at every crack.

"Yes, I was with a trainload of cattle," Boone agreed.

"You work for a big outfit, then?"

"The Moon Star," Boone replied shortly, and was surprised at Peabody's rejoinder.

"Moon Star, you say? That's Jeb Crowley's outfit, as I recall."

"That's right," Boone conceded.

He had a feeling that the questions were not idle conversation. Helen Hankinson spoke next. "Did you enjoy your trip to Chicago?"

"Well, I suppose I did," Boone replied, considering. It had meant a week's drive of the herd to the railroad, then several days of jolting in a caboose with the cattle train. He could think of more enjoyable journeys. "First time I'd ever been that far East."

A distant shout, a slowing of the coach, the blink of a light in the rain-wet night, indicated that they were at last pulling into Clayfield. Boone, one hand firmly clutching his bag, waited as the others crowded to alight. Inside the bag was ten thousand dollars, the cash receipts for the cattle he'd delivered to Chicago. He was supposed to pay the money over to another rancher in Clayfield, in exchange for a nice bunch of yearlings. Jeb Crowley liked to buy young stock and watch them grow into money.

A shadow loomed gigantic as the agent came from the station with a lantern in his hand. Someone jostled Boone as he descended, and a hard smash of a clubbed gun came at him from nowhere. Half seeing, partly sensing it, he ducked and jumped, and the blow was partially deflected. Even so, the gun barrel drove a new crease in his hat, at right angles to the one he regularly affected, and the numbing hammer on his skull sent him to his knees in the mud.

Hands wrenched at the bag, to which he clung doggedly. Then the light was at hand, people exclaiming, the confusion increasing as he was helped to his feet. Helen Hankinson was at his side, holding his other arm, steadying him. For the moment it was pleasant not to have to think. His head ached too much to make the effort.

Afterward came wonder and a measure of doubt. It seemed that no one had gotten a good look at his assailant, but Boone had a hunch that it must have been one of his fellow-passengers. Who else would guess that he carried enough money to be worth robbing?

For once he'd seen too little—or too much.

More than once it had been remarked that Boone Sarsfield was a "noticing" man; observant of small details which ordinarily went unseen. Now, as his horse snorted, for no apparent reason, and did an impromptu dance, he pulled it to a reluctant halt and looked about. The snort had been more than a gusty expelling of breath, though there was nothing to be seen, no varmint lurking in the grass. In fact, very little grass grew there; the ground was bare and dusty.

As he looked closely, the quality of the dirt excited his suspicion, even as some lingering odor, wafting up from it, had bothered his cayuse. Boone dismounted, kicking with the toe of his boot. Then he raked a spur experimentally through the soil, like a plow.

The double gesture was enough to disclose the reason for his horse's uneasiness. The ground, below a thin covering of dust, was not exactly muddy, but it had approached that consistency not long before. Now it was dark and unpleasant, a caked-together mass. Whatever he'd stumbled upon, he didn't like the look of it.

Homecoming had been less pleasant than he'd anticipated, beginning with that attempt to rob him in Clayfield. He'd paid the money over for the bunch of yearlings, according to orders, and had turned to find Peabody smiling crookedly at him.

"You're lucky," Peabody informed him. "From all accounts, you came close to losing that money last night." He added cryptically, "Probably you don't need any advice, Sarsfield. You strike me as a man able to look after himself. But any of us can get fooled at times. And that Bob Hankinson—I've known about him before. A no-good sort."

Peabody might be trying to cover up for himself, but the doubt he had implanted was a nagging one. There were a lot of things—

The clop-clop of hoofs brought him to attention; then, recognizing the oncoming pair of riders, he relaxed. This spot was close to a borderline, and a frontier for trouble. The newcomers, however, were men of Moon Star. Foremost, looming like a grizzly bear in the saddle, was Jeb Crowley. The boss of the Moon Star rode at a headlong pace. His companion, who gave a mistaken impression of sleepiness, was Crowley's friend and neighbor, Rusty Donovan, owner of Catclaw.

"What you found, Boone?" Crowley demanded. "Something wrong?"

"I'm wondering," Boone confessed. "My horse snorted, like he smelled something that didn't take his fancy. Something—or somebody—has done some bleeding here."

Crowley slid out of his saddle with characteristic promptness, his vast muscular body never seeming to be quite coordinated. He stared down at the patch of ground, stirring it in turn with his own boot toe. Donovan remained on his horse, his eyes all but closed, like a symbol of patience.

"Blood?" Donovan repeated dubiously.

"Ground's soaked with it," Crowley snapped. "Looks as though a calf, or maybe a yearling, had been butchered here, a night or so back. Whoever did it tried to smooth over the stain with fresh dirt, so's it wouldn't be noticed. Couldn't fool Boone, though."

"It was my horse did the noticing," Boone explained modestly. "He didn't like the smell."

"Well, I don't like it, either," Crowley snapped. "There's been a lot of little things lately that don't smell quite right, and I'm getting fed up." His gaze swept suspiciously toward the east and south, centering where a thin column of smoke arose, less than a mile away. Though the source of the smoke was concealed by a hill in between, all three men knew that it came from the shack of a homesteader.

Half a dozen nester families were clustered in that direction, sodbusters whose presence the ranchers had tolerated for about a year. But if proximity had brought familiarity, it had not increased liking. More and more, the settlers were regarded with hostility. Donovan's nose wrinkled beneath a heavy ruff of red hair.

"I can fair smell fryin' steak," he observed.

The remark was imaginative and suggestive. Always open to such stimulus, Crowley scowled.

"You figure it was a nester, helpin' himself to one of my herd?" he barked. "If I thought that—"

"Likely they're hungry," Donovan pointed out reasonably. "What else is there to eat?"

It was a logical question. Martin, the homesteader

from whose cabin the smoke rose, had proved a paragon of industry. For the first several weeks of occupancy, he and his family had lived in a tent, while he followed a plow from dawn to dusk. Unlike most of his fellow-settlers, he had gotten half a hundred acres in shape, then seeded the ground with winter wheat. Only after the crop was in had he taken time to haul lumber from Overcash's lumber mill near Singing River, a two-day round trip for each load. Then he had erected a cabin.

Fortune had seemed to smile on his industry. The crop had sprung green before the snows came, and by then, Martin's field had been enclosed with barbed wire. Under summer sun and rain, the shoots had climbed tall as a longhorn's hip.

When Sarsfield had ridden away behind the cattle, outbound for Chicago, the wheat's gold had matched that of the sun, with heads hanging heavy and ripe. The crop promised to be excellent, justifying not only Martin's faith but also all his hard work.

Then something had happened; ruin had come in a night. Boone had ridden past on his return and had had the story from others of the crew. They had awakened to the wild barking of a dog and beheld torch-like streamers flaring against the sky. Saddling hastily, they had been in time to check the advancing prairie fire before it could sweep Moon Star range or reach beyond to Catclaw. But the ripening wheat had been a total loss.

The other homesteaders, aroused, had also hurried to battle the flames, and in the lightening dawn, both parties of fire-fighters had viewed the others with sharpened distrust. There had been mutterings that the cattlemen had set fire to the grain, an accusation which Moon Star knew to be unjust. However great the provocation, Crawley had not yielded to that temptation.

Now, with Martin finding his crop destroyed and bare ground remaining, Donovan's question sounded logical. What was there for Martin and his family to eat, unless they helped themselves to a neighbor's beef?

"Reckon you can spare 'em an occasional steer, eh, Jeb? And so long as they stay content with one at a time—well, everybody knows you're big-hearted—even mebby a little soft-headed about such folks. Now I got to be getting back. See you later."

He swung his horse and was gone. Jeb Crowley swore. That final needling phrase had not been wasted.

"I've been a fool," he said bitterly, "toleratin' these darn nesters." He added thoughtfully, "Too long."

Boone Sarsfield was inclined to agree. Like the others of Moon Star's crew, he had been by turns surprised, bewildered and amazed that their employer should allow nesters to pre-empt land which Moon Star claimed, then to build houses and tear virgin sod with a plow. They had expected the hot-tempered Crowley to strike back with a cattleman's usual weapons—a warning, followed by threats; then force, enhanced by terror.

Such methods usually turned out to be no better than a holding operation, but in the majority of cases they bought time. By frightening off the first wave of settlers, they might keep others away, perhaps for a decade.

It had surprised no one that Rusty Donovan had counseled moderation, partly because Donovan's holdings were not yet threatened, and in part because Donovan was that type of man. Jeb Crowley, despite his hot-headedness, had taken the advice. He had been accustomed to listening to Donovan for nearly a quarter of a century.

They had been trail buddies, coming up the long road newly pioneered by Chisum. Hitting the country together, each had pre-empted an empire for himself. Returning to Texas to drive a herd north, they had stocked both ranges, and in the succeeding years they had prospered.

Only once had there been a serious threat to their friendship, when each had stubbornly refused to give way to the other as both courted the same girl. Surprisingly, once she had made her choice, Rusty

Donovan had proved to be a good loser. He'd congratulated Crowley, had even attended the wedding, and had continued to be a frequent caller on Moon Star. And when, little more than a year later, Jeb's bride had decamped with a cattle buyer, Donovan had been on hand to sympathize. In the succeeding years their friendship had strengthened.

Boone was familiar with the story, though all that had happened before his day. He'd been four years on Moon Star, but by comparison with most of the crew, he was a newcomer.

Clawing back into the saddle, Crowley was breathing hard. It was as though the distant smoke had gotten into his nostrils, the smoke of battle.

"Darn it, there's a limit," he exploded. "And I've reached it! I've tried to be decent and neighborly, lettin' them have their quarter-sections. But when those squatters start butcherin' my cattle, that's goin' too far. They've got to go."

Boone Sarsfield climbed back into his own saddle. Standing as tall as Crowley, he was lighter by thirty pounds, though on a horse the difference was less noticeable than afoot.

Crowley fired a sudden question at him. "That critter *was* butchered, wasn't it? No mistake there?"

"Must have been," Boone acknowledged. Had a wolf or puma feasted, there would have been less blood to soak into the ground, and remnants of bone and hide.

They rode for some minutes in silence, heading toward the buildings of Moon Star, Crowley deep in thought. Having made up his mind, he was never a man to lose time.

"I want them out of here, off this range, all of them," he pronounced. "I don't care how you do it, Boone. Take as many men as you figure you need, and evict them, every blasted nester. Do it tonight."

Though he had foreseen some such action in the offing, Boone was startled. Pratt Levinger was foreman at Moon Star, not himself. It was a mark of trust and favor to be singled out for such a task, as it had been to make the trip to Chicago, then return with the money the herd had brought. But this job was not to his liking. A year earlier, he'd have ridden as one of the crew to warn the nesters away, and thought little of it. But now—

A year could make changes in a man as well as in a country. There had been outrage on the faces of most of his fellows at sight of the broken sod, but Boone had sniffed the clean, earthly scent and found it not only reminiscent but delightful. The tingle of fresh earth had taken him back a dozen years, to the days when, a barefoot kid with a single gallus, he had followed his pa and the plow in spring. The overturned sod had been a springy carpet under bare foot, while blackbirds pranced along the rows, inspecting the job approvingly.

The rich green of the new wheat crop, showing in late fall, had twanged another forgotten chord of memory. He'd helped keep the cattle away from the all too frail fence, again on orders, though surprised that Jeb Crowley would go to such trouble on behalf of nesters who were enemies in a sense. He suspected that there was a streak of sentiment in Crowley, which the big man would have indignantly denied. Perhaps it had been increased by the sight of Martin's woman, standing slenderly proud, or digging among flowers by the side of the little house, walking tall in the scented dusk—

If those factors had moved Crowley, now he was angry and in a mood to brush them and the troublemakers aside indiscriminately. But Boone remembered. There were women in each house, also a few children. In the year of strained neighborliness, he'd met the men, and liked and respected them. They were hard-working and honest. That their dreams and ambitions clashed with those of the big landholders was regrettable, but understandable.

Thinking back, Boone understood. Helen Hankinson had reminded him of Laurie Martin. They didn't look alike, but in each was the same high, unconquered spirit, a gaiety which could laugh while tears blinked behind the lids—

He knew instinctively that Helen would not approve. And there was one more factor which Crowley might have overlooked. The wheat had burned just short of harvest. Such a fire did not happen by chance, and there had been no lightning. If Martin had butchered a calf, following the loss of his crop, he was hardly to be blamed.

"Might be a good idea to make sure first," Boone suggested.

"I'm sure of plenty," Crowley stormed. "Get them off."

Slowly Boone shook his head.

"I'd rather not."

Crowley swung to stare at him. "What's that?" he demanded, astounded. Men did not make a practice of gainsaying Jeb Crowley when he gave an order.

"Pick somebody else." Boone shrugged. "I couldn't drive those folks off."

Crowley's stare became a glare. The discovery that a calf, undoubtedly one of his, had been stolen and butchered had infuriated him. Once embarked on a course, he was never a man to cherish doubts, and it was his boast that he never turned back.

"Are you working for me?" he demanded ominously.

"Figured I was," Sarsfield agreed equably. This was a warning, and if he wanted to hang onto his job, he'd do well to heed it. The fact that he had been chosen for so important a job in preference to the foreman, or that he had been the one to discover the evidence of a rustling, would not count if he refused to obey an order.

Winter was on the way, and jobs were scarce. Also, in town, there was Helen Hankinson. He'd be a fool to risk losing his job, especially when others would execute the order, regardless.

"If you work for me, you do what I tell you," Crowley warned.

"Anything but that." Boone's head-shake was equally stubborn. "I wouldn't be good at such a job."

"Then you're no good for any job around here," Crowley snapped. "Draw your pay and ride!"

2.

Singing River, as a name for the town, was more poetic than accurate. In earlier days the stream which meandered past had been disparagingly called Coyote Creek, while the town had been known, not inappropriately, as Hardluck. Then a visiting schoolteacher, fresh from the East, had rechristened both, and the new names had stuck.

The town was some three dozen miles from the borders of Moon Star, and approximately an equal distance from the half-dozen homesteads which were the cause of Boone's present trouble. Sarsfield had more than once wondered why the settlers had come so far from town to encroach on Jeb Crowley's range, when equally good land had been available so much closer.

Now he shrugged as he sighted the town. The planned eviction of the nesters had been postponed past the previous evening because of his recalcitrance. In the early morning sunlight, Jeb Crowley had favored him with a hard, questioning stare, allowing him a last chance to change his mind. When he'd failed to avail himself of the opportunity, Crowley had paid over what wages he had coming and allowed him to ride out with no word of farewell.

He would spend the night at Singing River. Beyond that he had no plan, though he supposed he'd have to keep riding. The word would spread, so no one else would give him a job, even if they might have an opening. None of Crowley's neighbors would rashly incur his displeasure.

The boss of Moon Star could be generous, even magnanimous, when he was so minded. Conversely, he could be spiteful and unforgiving over a trifle. He liked to boast that, having embarked on a course, he never turned back.

It would be a wrench to leave this range, particularly Singing River, just as the Hankinsons were settling there. Still, he was probably deluding himself in even thinking that Helen Hankinson might take more than a casual interest in him; certainly she couldn't care for a jobless cowpuncher. Probably it was as well to get out now.

There was that nagging suspicion, already in his mind and further stimulated by Peabody's remark, concerning Helen's no-good brother. Perhaps that was one more reason he should keep riding.

Actually, Boone knew that, even if his suspicions

about Bob should be true, it wouldn't make any difference where his sister was concerned. It could be, Boone decided, that he was as stubborn-minded as Jeb Crowley.

There had been a white rime of frost when he'd set out, but the sun had soon melted it. Singing River baked in the glare of the September sun, belying its name. Dust puffed from under the hoofs of his horse, as Boone swung up to the high, wide-doored livery barn and rode into its hospitable gloom.

The long single street had been deserted as he rode along it. He dismounted, turning to view the grinning stable boy who advanced to take his horse. The flash of white teeth in a dark face recalled the morning frost on the blackened acres of Martin's ravished wheat field.

"Look after my horse, will you, Tom?" Boone requested. "He may have a long jaunt ahead, so give him a good feed of oats."

"Yessuh, Mistuh Sarsfield, I'll do that li'l thing," Tom Allard agreed. They had come to this range at about the same time, and he and Boone had been good friends ever since. "You sure likely to have some long jaunts, mos' any time now, for a fact. I'll take good care o' him, Mistuh Sheriff, yassuh!"

Boone stared in perplexity as Allard led the horse toward the far end of the long row of stalls. He started to call after him, then grinned and let it go. Tom was quite a hand for jokes.

Out on the street, he looked about, then turned toward the center of town. It could soon be encompassed; it consisted of a trio of saloons, a restaurant, the Hardluck Mercantile—which had never gotten around to changing its name—a blacksmith shop, the drugstore and a bank. There was a jail, but the long-proposed courthouse was still a dream, an all but faded gleam in the eyes of a few discouraged promoters. Such legal business as needed transacting was generally taken care of in one of the saloons.

He was passing the Merc when a man stepped from it, stared an instant, then hailed him warmly.

"Well, dog my cats, you're mighty prompt on the job today, Sheriff!"

Boone surveyed him carefully. Eb Callendar was the blacksmith, but not an ordinary one. He always found time for pranks, and it struck Boone that this must be one of them.

Certainly it was too early in the afternoon for him to be drunk.

"Sheriff?" he repeated. "Purdy is sheriff."

Callendar gave an airy gesture with one big hand. "Levitious Purdy *was* sheriff," he acknowledged, "but no longer. Since and as of ten o'clock last night, you are the sheriff of Singing River."

Boone sighed. "I didn't think anyone could get so soused so early in the afternoon," he reproved.

"Drunk? My friend, you do me an injustice—but likewise you give me an idea. Not once this day have I washed the dust from my throat, which is a condition that should be remedied. Favor me by stepping inside one of our emporiums of thirst. It will be my pleasure to buy a drink for our new custodian of the law."

"The way your tongue hangs in the middle and wags at both ends, you missed your calling," Boone commented. "Only trouble is, you talk a lot and say mighty little." He followed Callendar into the nearest saloon.

"Ain't it the truth!" Callendar agreed. "With my gift for gab, I should have been a law sharp, or at the least a sky pilot. Perhaps a politician. You are now elevated to that class, as sheriff of the county."

"There you go again," Boone reproved him. "What's this about being sheriff? Me, I'm just a cowpuncher—or I was."

"You were, but now you're the wearer of the tin star. As of yesterday afternoon, Leviticus Purdy ceased being the custodian of the law in this our midst. He was detected in an act unbecoming the wearer of the badge—to wit, nefariously accepting a bribe, in cash, to turn loose a prisoner, without trial or due process of law. The citizenry were duly shocked, not to say outraged."

"I suppose it would have been all right if he had merely turned the man loose without being paid for it?"

"Oh, of course and indubitably," Callendar agreed. "Such is a sheriff's privilege. But when he looses a prisoner for a fee, illegally paid—well, we could not condone such conduct. We prevailed upon him to resign, then applied tar and a dusting from a feather pillow, and gave him a ride out of town, he astraddle a rail. In other words, if not Godspeed, at least we provided him with a speedy take-off."

Boone sensed that the man was serious. Gradually the details came out. There had been a large gathering in town the previous afternoon, of men with leisure on their hands, a few too many drinks under their belts, and a yen for a good time. Apparently the affair had been abetted by Callendar, but Boone gathered that someone else, who had largely kept in the background, had been the real instigator of the affair. It had started out as a search for fun, taking the outward semblance of horseplay. Apparently there had been some pretext of justice. The unpopular and incompetent sheriff had been caught accepting a bribe, then treated as described.

Since the crowd had been hilariously drunk, and without a single member of Moon Star's crew among them, Purdy had probably gotten off easily.

There were undercurrents here which Boone was quick to sense. Moon Star, and Moon Star's boss, would not have approved, had they known. Such a thing could not have been done save under the stimulus of liquor and the guise of fun. But had it been in fun?

It had occurred to the merry-makers, in a state both exalted and hilarious, that since they had caused the office to be vacated, it was logically up to them to fill it again. Various names had been suggested, but none had met with favor until Callendar had put forth Boone Sarsfield. Whether they were too drunk to think straight, or had belatedly desired to appease Crowley by the choice of one of his men, the nomination had met with favor. Boone had been elected by universal acclamation.

"So, since ten o'clock last evening, you are the duly elected sheriff of the county," Callendar added. "And let me be the first to congratulate you."

This far, Boone had listened with amused tolerance. Now he shook his head reprovingly.

"Yesterday you may have been drunk, Eb. Today you're sober, and as an intelligent man, you know that this whole thing is ridiculous."

"What's ridiculous about it?" Callendar challenged. "Purdy resigned, and he's out. No question about that."

"That may be, but the election of a successor is something else. Your horseplay has no legal standing."

"A majority of the voters were present, and all

were in favor of you," Callendar pointed out. "And shall not the will of the people prevail? Anyhow, it was legal enough. Judge Vanklyber was in town, which doesn't often happen. He agreed that an emergency existed, the office of sheriff being vacant and needing to be filled. So he certified yesterday afternoon for a special election, and afterward he signed the certificate of election, which makes it legal and binding."

Vanklyber, whose territory as district judge encompassed three large counties, visited Singing River periodically. From what little he knew of him, Boone could appreciate the probability that the judge might go along with such a proposition, to give it the stamp of legality. He'd wink at the ousting of an incompetent and manifestly dishonest sheriff, rather than incur the displeasure of the crowd to no good end.

"Where's the judge now?"

"Long gone. He rode out early this morning."

That appeared to finalize it; the transfer of authority might indeed be legal. Judge Vanklyber, he had gathered, had not particularly approved of Purdy, but he was too shrewd a politician to antagonize knowingly so powerful an outfit as Moon Star. Approving the selection of one of Moon Star's crew had no doubt seemed to him a good solution.

The trouble was that there were factors of which the judge, and possibly some others had been ignorant. Now, instead of being out of a job, Boone was suddenly in the middle of a new one—if he chose to accept it.

Apparently his arrival in town had been noted. Others were beginning to enter the saloon, pressing forward to shake his hand and add their congratulations. Clearly this was not a joke, however it might have started out. One man came with the star, the legal badge of office. He reached to pin it on Boone's shirt, and the others cheered.

Boone surveyed them soberly. Whether the joke was on them or on himself he was by no means certain. One fact surprised him. He was better liked in the community than he'd ever suspected. Even now, on the day after the election, most of these people were pleased with their choice.

But there was more here than most of them might suspect. Purdy had proved a disappointment, and there had been little law or order while he was sheriff. Thus it probably seemed to them that the job was not very important. The whole thing had started out as a joke, but it could be a job—if he cared to take it.

That, however, could decidedly prove a cayuse of another color. By now the room, which had been almost empty, was crowded to capacity. Among the late-comers were men he had regarded as friends, sober-minded citizens who, whatever their condition the night before, were sober now.

"Reckon we went a mite far," one acknowledged,

while the others fell silent. "It seemed like a good idea at the time. But of course being sheriff ain't no joke. . . . Could be that the sensible thing, as far as you're concerned, would be to go back to the ranch and keep on where you are, Boone."

That could have been sound advice, except for one thing.

"I don't work there any more," he informed them. "Crowley fired me."

"Fired you? Jeb did? What you giving us?"

"We didn't see eye to eye," Boone explained briefly.

There was a momentary silence while that was digested, and the others eyed him and themselves uneasily. Even the ebullient Callendar could understand the implications. If Jeb Crowley had fired him, then he would not take kindly to finding his cast-off hand in the position of sheriff, with his favored one having been summarily removed.

And, despite Judge Vankliyber, such law as there had been, or was, lay in the word of Jeb Crowley. Under the circumstances, he might not merely not approve, but might strongly disapprove of the election and its choice.

"Looks like maybe we got carried away," Callendar acknowledged. "I hate to admit it, Boone, but I guess we sort of did."

What he was actually suggesting was that, in view

of this new knowledge, Boone should keep riding, clear out of the county. Boone glanced down at the star pinned to his shirt. The sight gave him a strange feeling. That badge represented the law—and, joke or not, the former sheriff had quit and fled the country, and he had been elected. To be sheriff—he'd always thought of that as the most important office in the country, a position of responsibility and trust—

On the other hand, what Callendar was implying made a lot of sense. There were hidden factors behind all this. More to the point, Jeb Crowley was a good friend, when he was on your side. Offended, he was a bad enemy, and Moon Star wielded a big influence in the county. Backed by Catclaw, Crowley had a way of running things.

Considering their personal clash, Jeb would almost certainly be displeased with this more or less mock election, though the participants had expected to gain his approval. The changes of a night could make all the difference.

Should he stay, under these circumstances, and try to wear the star, Boone knew that he'd be asking for trouble, and plenty of it. On the other hand—

A voice spoke unexpectedly from the edge of the crowd. Word of what was happening had spread across the town. Boone started, but the surprise was pleasurable, for it was Helen Hankinson's voice.

"Don't you quit, Boone Sarsfield! You were fairly

elected sheriff—I saw and heard what went on. You're the sheriff now, and you can do the job, and the Good Lord knows that a real man is needed in that position! You can show them. Why don't you?"

Helen had climbed on to a chair, so that her slender figure towered above the shoulders of the rest of the crowd. Apparently she had already adopted Singing River, making it her town. There could be no doubt that she meant what she said. In her he had a believer and a champion.

There was momentary silence while others turned to look, some without recognition, others surprised or outraged that a woman should interfere in men's business. Some were admiring, others somewhat appalled. One of the latter voiced a challenge.

"You're anxious to get him killed, girl?"

Helen's face paled, showing that she had heard of his fall from favor at Moon Star, and apparently understood the implications as well as anyone. Then color, born at least partly of anger, flooded back into her cheeks.

"Killed, did you say? Who's talking about being killed? You elected him, and he's the sheriff now. And you've all agreed that the county needs a sheriff, a man who can do the job. Well, I'm not afraid to state that I think Boone Sarsfield is that man. So go ahead and do it, Boone. Show them!"

It was a wildly improbable situation, born of a

drunken jest, but Boone Sarsfiéld found his blood quickening to the challenge. Moreover, Helen was there, and that made a tremendous difference. It was this job or none. Moreover, he'd never been one for running or being pushed around. Helen's eyes were flashing, darkly challenging. It was strange that he hadn't really noticed before how pretty she was.

"Since you put it that way," he agreed, "you folks have got yourselves a sheriff!"

3.

A shocked silence followed his pronouncement. The crowd who had jammed into the saloon eyed him uncertainly, and it came to Boone that in their minds the whole affair had actually been only a hilarious joke, the product of too much alcohol. Most of the congratulations extended to him today had been a carry-over from yesterday's mood.

That he might take any of it seriously had been outside their calculations. Apparently the action of the judge in confirming the election had not registered with most of them. They had hardly been in a condition to understand.

"Good for you!" Helen applauded. "That's telling them!" Then, as she realized her position, a fresh wave of color suffused her face, and she jumped down from the chair, darting out the door. After a moment Boone followed, in a still profound silence.

He was in time to see her disappearing into The Red Rooster Restaurant, and on impulse he followed.

He was hungry, and he wanted to see her again.

At that hour the place was empty. He looked around for Helen at a table or on a stool by the counter, then understood as she came from the kitchen, tying an apron in place. Characteristically, she had lost no time finding a job and going to work, after reaching town.

Her color was still high as she looked at him, but she met his regard calmly.

"I'm glad you took it," she said. "From all reports, a real sheriff is badly needed here."

Boone eyed her with increasing interest. Women were not allowed to vote, though a few of the bolder ones were declaring that they should be allowed to do so, insisting that they could do at least as well as did the men. If she was a fair sample, he was inclined to agree. She was concerned with the needs of the community and the functions of the office, which was more than could be said for most of the men who had so hilariously cast their votes for him.

"This comes as a surprise to me," he confessed. "But I find it rather intriguing." He grinned. "And it's been a long while since I ate."

"We can remedy that, at least," she promised, and disappeared into the kitchen. He heard a sound of vigorous shaking and poking at the fire in the range, then the spatter of frying eggs and ham in a skillet. When she returned and placed the platter before him, she eye him curiously.

"That's an unusual word," she observed. "Intriguing. One seldom hears it."

It was now Boone's turn to color. "Aw, I guess that one was left over from when I was a kid," he protested. "I don't make a practice of using four-dollar words."

"You do, though, every now and then," she returned seriously. "Maybe you don't even think about it, but it's easy to tell that you've had an education. I think that's wonderful—especially now that you're sheriff."

"Might help me to persuade some outlaw not to shoot at me." He grinned. "Sort of overwhelm him with talk. Do you like this job?"

"It's fine," she replied. "And there's not too much choice around here. With Bob gone so much of the time—"

She broke off, biting her lip, but her glance did not waver. Boone sought to cover her confusion.

"It's nice to know that I have one friend and wellwisher, anyhow," he said, pushing back from the counter. "That helps."

"Oh, I'm quite sure that almost everybody is your friend," she assured him earnestly. "I've overheard quite a bit of talk. It's just that they didn't really take the election seriously. Most of them were really lit up last evening. But they meant well, and I'm sure they wish you well. It bothered them when they realized what they might be getting you in to. Is Mr. Crowley such an ogre?"

"Jeb? Shucks, no. He's sort of headstrong at times, but he means well."

"He trusted you to handle a lot of money for him. So he must think well of you."

Apparently several people had known that he carried that money, when the attempt had been made to rob him. That it might have become common knowledge was disturbing, but he brushed the thought aside.

"Jeb and I always got along fine, long as I took his orders. When we couldn't quite see eye to eye, that was that."

But it wasn't quite so simple as he made it sound. When he returned to the street, the town had resumed its normal activities. If many of the crowd had gone to the saloon with the notion of having another convivial round by way of celebration, the news that he had been fired from Moon Star had driven such thoughts from their minds.

He shoved open the door to the sheriff's office, looking around curiously. He had never been inside it before, and the room was eloquent of his predecessor's indolent ways. A not often disturbed coating of dust was on everything but the chair, and cobwebs swayed lazily from the ceiling. A cot was against one wall, a rusty heating stove near the center of the room, its sides adorned with dried tobacco juice. A battered desk occupied another wall, the roll-top half open, a dusty collection of papers protruding from cubbyholes. Nails driven in the wall above held a couple of rings of keys. Another door stood open on the dim recesses of the cell-block beyond.

Boone threw open the window, then tried the chair. It creaked as he settled his weight in it. On the desk lay a legal-looking document, and he picked it up, then read it with increasing interest. It was the certificate of election, apparently placed there by Judge Vanklyber before his departure, and duly signed by him.

Another glance completed the inventory of the room. A half-empty water bucket was on a stand in one corner, with a rusty dipper floating on it. A battered Stetson and old coat hung by pegs on the wall, personal property which his predecessor had lacked either the time or the inclination to retrieve. Two straight-backed chairs sat against the wall.

In the adjoining room, Boone eyed the cells, finding all four empty. At least there were no prisoners suffering for lack of attention. He returned to the outer air, liking the feel of the late afternoon sun. The entire place would require a lot of cleaning and mopping, a thorough airing, before he'd feel comfortable, or consider the jail fit for the incarceration of prisoners.

From long instinct, he turned to gaze at the horizon, and stiffened. On so cloudless a day, it was possible to see a long way.

Off whence he had come, smoke arose like signals, mounting high. He guessed that in volume it must match the billowing clouds when Paul Martin's wheat had gone up in a crimson tide, only a few days before.

Yet today there was a difference. It was easy to tell these smoke clouds came from half a dozen different sources. At such a distance, it would be easy to consider them all as one single smudge, but Boone knew better. There was no longer a big field of dead-ripe grain, with torch-dry straw, to produce such a cloud. The columns of smoke could come only from the burning buildings of the six homesteaders.

Though he had been prepared for such an eventuality, the sight was still shocking. Jeb Crowley had made a threat, and Crowley was a man who carried out his warnings. There had been a few hours of delay, due to Boone's refusal to be the instrument of such a vendetta, but it was clear that, once he had departed, Crowley had lost no time in putting his plan into operation.

Last evening, Boone had been disheartened at the prospect, his thoughts and then his dreams troubled by the misery which it would bring to the six families. It was worse than it once would have been, in that they had been allowed to stay on their land for over a year, and thus had been given tacit encouragement. Crowley had permitted them to plow and plant, to haul lumber and erect houses, to do the thousand things, little or great, which went into the making of a home.

Now such destruction, with winter in the offing, was a thousand times worse than it would have been to turn them away at gun-point.

Boone had registered his protest against the idea by quitting, but even that morning, the whole situation had remained somewhat impersonal. He had always been on the side of the cattlemen, and there had not been much that he could do.

All at once it was different. He was the sheriff, and though no oath to uphold the law had been administered, he understood the duties attendant upon the office. The law was being violated, legal settlers evicted at gun-point.

Now this was his business.

That his former employer was the instrument of injustice should not be allowed to make a difference. Yet the truth of the matter was that it would probably make a lot.

Apparently the crew of Moon Star had waited awhile after evicting the settlers before putting their buildings to the torch. The homesteaders must have been on the road throughout most of the day, not many miles behind himself on the way to town. Already, nearing the edge of Singing River, a caravan was coming into sight. It seemed made up of misery and dejection, anger and impotent grief. There were six wagons, piled high with such possessions as could be loaded.

Escorting the evicted families were half the crew of Moon Star, a dozen watchful men, with revolvers at their sides and rifles in their hands.

On this day there had been a change in the established pattern. Almost always, for a score of years, when any important action took place, it had been a joint effort of Moon Star and Catclaw. Today it was Moon Star alone, not a solitary rider from the big neighboring outfit lending even tacit support to the operation.

Even on the road the separation persisted. Not too far behind his crew and the wagons they escorted, Jeb Crowley rode toward Singing River. But Rusty Donovan, although heading for the same destination, was not with him. Donovan rode by himself, keeping back from the road, on the far fringes of the fields. Had there been anyone to see, it must have struck them as odd, if not significant.

Boone Sarsfield watched glumly as the caravan approached. Not much imagination was required to picture what had happened; how each family, busy with morning chores or perhaps in the middle of breakfast, had been surprised by the arrival of an armed deputation, a couple of grim-faced men with guns in hand. They had been brusquely ordered to hitch up teams, to load what possessions they could onto the wagon, and then to get out.

Almost certainly there had been tears and pleas, imprecations and threats, to all of which the riders from Moon Star had been equally deaf. The men might not relish their task, but they carried out orders. The summary firing of Sarsfield would insure that.

With each homestead threatened, there had been nowhere for any of the settlers to turn for assurance, no possibility of help. Any who refused to obey would be harshly dealt with.

In retrospect, it was significant that Crowley, giving

Boone an order the day before, then repeating it today, had not been troubled by any possibility that the law might hinder such a plan. Crowley had been certain that Leviticus Purdy would be on his side, or at least that he would remain carefully neutral.

Having had a year in the country to learn what sort of a man filled the office, the homesteaders, too, would understand the futility of any appeal to the law.

Had it been coincidence that Purdy had been so suddenly removed from his position on the eve of the action by Crowley?

Now all those who had come with high hopes the year before were to be herded through the town, then on out of the country. It was an exhibition calculated to break any spirit of resistance which might remain, as well as to serve as a warning to others who might be thinking of finding land. There was planned purpose in such brutality.

The foremost wagon was piled high, as though hastily loaded. Bedding, mattresses, clothing, household utensils, a plow, all made a discouraged pile. A brown hen perched on a chair rung, teetering precariously as the chair swayed to the jolting of the wagon.

Paul Martin was driving, shoulders stiffly erect, yet his defiant mien was belied by a spot near the corner of his mouth which worked in helpless anger. Beside him, Laurie Martin sat rigidly, her face shaded under a starched sunbonnet, looking neither to the right or left. The Martins had no children.

There were children on the other wagons, some crying, all looking lost and bewildered. None of the cows which belonged to the homesteaders had been brought along. They could not travel at such a pace, and had not been allowed. Only the horses plodded steadily, as though such a thing were routine.

People were appearing at doorways along the street, looking out with surprise. Some clearly approved; others apparently did not like what they saw, but knew better than to interfere. Everyone recognized the brand of Moon Star on the horses; its crescent was as merciless toward its enemies as the sword of the Prophet. For most people, the chief element of wonder was that this eviction had been so long in coming.

Boone's jaws tightened; then, as the first wagon approached, he walked to the middle of the street and halted. Martin, a flash of hope lighting his eyes, perforce pulled his team to a stop. The others behind him followed suit as a matter of course.

Luke Lucas, mounted on a pinto still frisky at day's end, eyed Boone with surprise. Of all the crew with whom Boone had worked these last several years, Lucas had come closest to being a friend. That morning, it had been in his mind to extend his hand and speak a word of farewell, but he'd glanced instead at his fellows, then had restrained the impulse.

At the stopping of the wagon, Mrs. Martin looked up quickly. It occurred to Boone that she had been riding with her eyes tightly closed, a proud spirit shrinking before the stare of curious or hostile eyes. She saw the badge on his shirt, and her eyes widened. Then she leaned forward, an eager desperation in her voice.

"You are the sheriff?" Doubt came briefly, with partial recognition that she had seen him before, and on Moon Star. "Can't you do something, sir? We are being driven from our homes—illegally, at gunpoint—"

Pratt Levinger came spurring from where he had ridden near the rear. Anger burned in his eyes; always light brown, they now resembled the fierce yellow of a hawk's. Amazement and disbelief churned with other emotions in his face at the sight of Sarsfield and the badge which he wore.

"What the devil?" Levinger ejaculated. "What are you doing here? What are you about, Boone?"

Sarsfield shrugged. He'd never had much liking for Pratt Levinger, but the man was capable, and he placed his employer's interests ahead of everything else, as he was paid to do.

"The question seems to be what *you're* about," Boone returned. "This strikes me as a pretty high-handed proceeding. Also, of course, it's outside the law."

"What's the law got to do with it?" Levinger demanded. "And how come you're wearing that star?"

"They gave it to me, as sheriff. Seems that Purdy quit the job, and a special election was held yesterday. I wasn't here then, of course, and didn't know anything about it, but I was elected."

"The devil you were!" Levinger exclaimed unbelievingly. He took a moment to digest that, staring at the star, controlling his dancing cayuse with a tight hand on the reins. Most of the others who were serving as escort to the wagons came up, loosely grouped, but watchful and very alert. Their amazement at the piece of information equaled Levinger's, and was coupled with even greater skepticism.

"Such an election wouldn't hold." The foreman shrugged. "In any case, don't interfere with our business."

"Maybe that's your opinion, Pratt, but the majority says otherwise. Let's have no misunderstanding. I'm wearing the star and speaking as the law. Keep that in mind, for you've already overstepped the bounds of the law. As sheriff, I've no choice but to take a hand."

The others had grown watchfully silent, displaying varying degrees of expectancy. Levinger shrugged again. There was much here which he didn't understand, but it didn't really matter. The law in this county had always been Moon Star, and so it would continue to be.

"I don't buy that," he warned flatly. "And you're crazy if you do. Just what do you think you're going to do?" Tauntingly he added, "What do you think you *can* do?"

Boone inhaled a slow breath. None of this was of his planning or seeking, but at such a time you didn't back down.

"What I do will depend on you. In the name of the law, you will cease and desist from interfering with these people. Call off your crew and head back where you belong."

The eyes which glared back at him were fierce and defiant. Boone had seen the same look in the eyes of a wolf surprised above a slain calf.

"There's been enough foolishness," Levinger pronounced tartly. "We're escortin' these folks out of the country. *Get out of the way!*"

For the moment, this was between himself and Levinger. The rest of the crew of Moon Star would not interfere unless it seemed necessary, and they were sure that Levinger could handle the situation. That was why he was foreman for Jeb Crowley, a man both able and willing to handle whatever came along.

The onlookers would remain merely spectators, each for his own personal reason, but in the main because they were afraid to do otherwise. Most of them had voted for Boone Sarsfield for sheriff only the day before, but at the time it had seemed a huge joke, even if they didn't quite understand the point of it. Certainly none had envisioned any such situation when shouting their approval.

It was one thing to elect a member of Moon Star's crew, who would have the approval and backing of the big outfit. It was something entirely different for Moon Star to be lined up against the man. Few in the crowd considered a tin star as even remotely equal to the Moon Star.

A block down the street, standing in the doorway of The Red Rooster, Boone glimpsed Helen. She too was watching, and she would be on his side. Nonetheless it was a lonely place to stand.

"I'll give you a final warning," Boone said. "Don't interfere with the law!"

"The devil with the law—and you!" Levinger spat contemptuously. "And what are you going to do about it?"

"First I'm arresting you," Boone returned. "Step down, with your arms in the air."

He moved ahead as he gave the orders, arms swinging at his sides. The air seemed all at once to hold the menace of a coming storm. Pratt Levinger stared down incredulously. Boone could almost read his thoughts. Such law as there had been in the country had been at the will of Moon Star, with the backing of Catclaw. Whether or not the holder of the office of sheriff was a figurehead had not mattered. Between them, the two big outfits were dominant, and only a fool or a crazy man ever tried to dispute them.

Levinger had been certain that Boone was bluffing. that in a showdown he would be sensible enough to realize how hopeless would be his opposition. Of course he had to make a picture, as a face-saving move. Beyond that, he would never dare go.

Laurie Martin cried out sharply. For as Boone continued to walk toward him, Pratt Levenger was going for his gun.

He'd slipped the Winchester back into his saddle sheath as he rode to the front of the line, arrogantly certain that it would not be needed. Now, realizing that he'd miscalculated, that Boone Sarsfield intended to do exactly what he said and place him under arrest, Levinger reacted in the only way he knew. Since Boone was forcing a showdown, let the consequences be upon his own head.

Levinger's Colt was out and spitting lead as Boone cleared the last several feet in a sudden leap. At most times in the past, even the day before, in a similar situation, he'd have gone for his own gun, trying to reach it first. The odds had shifted when he'd accepted the star now glittering on his shirt-front.

A move for his own gun would mean that Moon Star would back Levinger with theirs. From them there were only blacks and whites, with no grays, no sharps or flats in the situation. War was war, and you fought to win.

But to draw on a man who kept his own weapon holstered was something else. For Pratt, of course, the situation was different. He was threatened, therefore justified. And since he was drawing, he could handle the situation, and adequately.

So they believed, and the same certainly was in Levinger. Only something was wrong, and nothing was going as he had calculated or intended. It had been surprising that Boone Sarsfield had quit his job, defying Jeb Crowley and an order received, and it was even more astounding to find Sarsfield wearing the star of the law. Yet all of that paled into insignificance compared with the defiance of himself and Moon Star.

Levinger emptied the gun, at point-blank range, and it was a measure of how shaken he was that he should miss. Not that Boone was standing still to offer an easy target. His giant leap, sidewise as well as forward, was disconcerting. Men didn't usually jump toward a gun. Then the gun was empty, and Boone's hands were reaching. One closed on Levinger's gun wrist, and the other found his belt. With a heave and twist, he threw the foreman on the ground, and the sheriff's gun was menacing the others who had ridden as escort for the wagons.

5.

Sarsfield's voice carried clearly in the sudden hush.

"I'm giving the orders. Hands away from guns. If any of you try any tricks, you may get me, but Levinger will die at the same time!"

Men all but ceased to breathe, their doubts erased. The impossible had happened, and it created a new certainty in place of the old. At that moment, none of them had any doubt that he could accomplish what he threatened.

"You're crazy," Levinger protested. His hands rose jerkily, the redness of rage battling a sudden flabbiness in his cheeks. It had been years since any man had dared challenge Moon Star, or himself as its representative. He wondered if he was getting soft, and the doubt echoed in his voice. "You can't get away with this, Boone."

"You said that before. Now, let everybody get a couple of things straight. I'm the sheriff of this county, duly elected, and that election has been certified by Judge Vanklyber." He paused, to allow that to sink in.

"This thing that you've done today, Pratt, is not only an outrage, evicting these people by force, but it's outs—"

"Are you sidin' with nesters?" Levinger snarled.

"Calling them nesters doesn't change the situation. They've all filed on land owned not by Moon Star or Catclaw, but by the government. The homestead act gives them a right to settle on that land, live on it and prove up, after which it becomes their land, guaranteed to them by Uncle Sam. Don't try to buck the government!"

"Listen to him!" Levinger jeered. "You missed your calling. You should have been a law shark!"

Boone sensed, as did Levinger, that the crowd was behind him, their attitude subtly altered. There were several reasons for the change, not the least being a sense of pride in this man who both proclaimed and upheld the law—and for whom they had voted.

"Don't interfere with the law," Boone added, "nor with these folks, not any more. Pratt, march ahead of me."

Pratt, with a gun at his back, had no choice but to move across to the sheriff's office. Boone checked a gusty sigh of relief when the door closed behind them. It was impossible to keep an eye on his prisoner and watch the crowd at the same time, and he'd subconsciously been braced again the smash of a leaden slug between his shoulder blades. One bullet could retrieve the situation for the Moon Star. Sarsfield might live long enough to hear the blast from the gun, and there was a possibility that he could make good on his own threat to take Pratt Levinger with him on the dim trail beyond Boot Hill.

Yet if he did that much, the man who regained control for Moon Star would receive the approbation of Jeb Crowley; moreover, there would be a vacancy to fill in the foremanship.

No one had quite dared chance it. Boone reached for the key ring above the desk, urging his reluctant prisoner along the corridor to the cell block. He found it a clumsy task to try one key after another, working one-handed, to get a door open. Why the cells had been kept locked, when no one was inside, he could not understand.

He sensed the tenseness of desperation in his prisoner, and growled a warning. Levinger relaxed, and the next key opened the lock. "Inside," Boone ordered, then blanched at the nauseating stench. Levinger, always a fastidious man, protested.

"This place is worse than a hog pen. You'll not keep me in here—it ain't decent."

"I gave you a choice before I arrested you," Boone reminded him wearily. "I agree that it's filthy, but that's not my fault. I've had no time or chance to clean it up since takin' over. But at least it's a shelter. You can reflect on the way you've been burning the homes of decent people, and decide if you deserve anything better."

"Heck, man, do you think I relished that job?" Levinger protested. "I hadn't—" He caught himself sharply.

"You had a choice, same as I did," Boone pointed out, and locked the door, pocketing the keys. When he returned to the street, the sun was low on the horizon, the day all but done. It had been eventful, but it was still far from over. He sensed that as he saw a horseman come at a gallop, and recognized the massive figure of his former employer.

Crowley had left the chores to his foreman, then had headed to town to make sure that nothing went wrong. Sensing now that something was amiss, he was losing no time.

A couple of his crew rode to meet him, and they pulled up for a parley. The others, who had escorted the evicted homesteaders at gun-point, milled about, waiting expectantly. The six wagons remained where they had halted.

It did not take long to explain the situation. Catching sight of Boone, Crowley rode straight to where he waited. He stared arrogantly a moment before swinging down from his horse and dropping the reins. More than ever he had the aspect of a grizzly bear.

"I've been hearing some surprising news," he observed, his tone deceptively mild. "Sort of interesting, though. So you're wearing a star now, Boone?"

"I'm wearing one," Boone agreed.

The quality of the answer left Crowley momentarily taken aback. There could be no question that Sarsfield was doing exactly that.

"You've got more guts than I gave you credit for," Crowley admitted, "but a darned sight less sense!"

"You should have been around long enough to get some sense of your own, Jeb," Boone returned. "Enough to know that you can't get away with that sort of thing."

It was the wrong retort. If Crowley had suffered any compunctions during the day, or entertained doubts as to the wisdom of his course, still he had embarked upon it. Having boasted that he never turned back after making up his mind, to him there could be no possible reversal.

Worse, his former employee was questioning his judgment. Of late years he had allowed no one to do that.

"You callin' me a fool?" he growled. "We'll see who's the fool!"

He lunged at Boone, striking out with a massive swing of balled fist, confident of ending the fight with the one blow. Boone was aware of the power in that arm, and what it might do if it connected. Knowing

Crowley, he'd been tensed for such a strike, without warning.

He moved to the side, grabbing the fist in both his hands. Utilizing Crowley's rush, he spun, lifting, completing a full circle. When he let go, the combined force sent Crowley hurtling through the air, to bring up with a crash against the side of the sheriff's office.

Crowley sprawled a moment in a grotesque huddle, badly shaken. Then he reared suddenly to his feet, shaking his head, and charged headlong a second time.

This time, however, he had learned caution. He checked his rush, kicking out with his left foot as treacherously as a mule, the boot aimed to cripple. No brutality was barred in the school in which he'd been trained.

Again Boone grabbed, but this time he missed. The heel of the boot scraped his hip, staggering him. Instantly Crowley was on him.

The next few minutes were a nightmare, confused at the time and never afterward straight in Boone's mind. Back and forth they moved over the full width of the street, slugging, going down, then coming to their feet, a savage melee before which even hardened bystanders gave way. One factor began gradually to assume significance. Jeb Crowley, who had never lost a battle, was holding his own, but only that.

Boone knew that he had to keep out of the grip of

those big paws. Once they obtained a hold, they would remain as relentless as a bulldog's jaws. Twice he slugged savagely as Crowley tried to get a hold, driving the big man back. Once he stomped hard with his heel at the toe of Crowley's boot, and once he drove a knee to the groin.

This was a question of survival, not merely for himself but for the homesteaders in whose behalf he had intervened, and in the final analysis for the community itself, for law and decency. Gradually the assurance came to him that even such a man as Crowley could be whittled down to size.

Boone hadn't sought this fight, but he'd never been one to back away from trouble. That had been Crowley's first mistake, the assumption that Sarsfield was backing away the day before. Now it was beginning to dawn on Crowley that he'd made a bad mistake.

The realization increased his anger, the bitter determination to smash this man. The possibility of losing did not occur to him. He never lost. If there was any likelihood that he might, his crew would take a hand.

It was occurring to some of them that there was more than a possibility that Sarsfield might beat Crowley, even as he had overcome Levinger. In his years on Moon Star, Boone had never been tested in quite this fashion. He'd been a quiet man, deceptively so, and they had underestimated him.

That belonged to the past. He was on the opposite side of the fence now. One man, dismounted, started to make a move to assure victory for his employer. Not much should be required; merely the thrust of a foot at a critical moment to trip the sheriff, send him sprawling in the path of merciless boots—

A voice cut sharply above the lesser sounds, attracting the attention of the onlookers.

"Mister, you try that sort of thing, and I'll let daylight through you!"

The crewmen jerked about, startled, then shrank back. Helen Hankinson had mounted the three steps to the post-office. From that vantage-point she commanded a fine view, and her position was improved by a double-barreled shotgun, held at the ready.

Luck could be two-sided. Not only did the watchers turn at her voice, but so did Crowley and Boone. For Boone, it was almost a fatal error. He stepped on a round stone, embedded in the dirt, and his feet went out from under him as if he had been jerked. It was precisely the result which the crewman had hoped to achieve.

Crowley saw him go down and jumped. This was the classical method of ending a fight: smashing down on a helpless opponent with both feet. Should a man survive, it would be as a cripple.

Rolling desperately, Boone twisted and grabbed. One spurred foot raked his side, but his other arm found a hold, and he heaved desperately. The fact he had gotten hold of but one leg proved both a handicap and an asset. For the onlookers, what followed was almost too sudden to comprehend.

Crowley's massive bulk refused to spill, but something had to give. There was a sharp snap, the sound audible to everyone, and the boss of Moon Star collapsed, the bone in his leg cleanly broken.

6.

To save himself by spilling his opponent had been Boone's intent, but the result was an unplanned accident, so completely unexpected that everyone was caught by surprise, Crowley most of all. He lay a moment in the freshly stirred dust of the street, face down and twisted in a grimace of agony. Then he tried to roll, to defend himself from the boot-jumping retaliation he expected, the follow-up he would have pursued had the advantage been with him.

The effort sent an added shock of agony through him, and that was too much. As ingloriously, in his own eyes, as a woman, Crowley fainted.

Breathing heavily, Boone struggled upright, gazing at Crowley, estimating what had happened. The condition of the limb was not hard to judge, since it was turned now at an unusual angle. Crowley would live to fight another day, but for the moment, Boone's attention could be turned to more important matters.

His shirt was hanging by a strip of collar, the rest of it torn away. His face felt like a well-rounded beefsteak, and he had no doubt that the resemblance extended also to his appearance. But the important thing was that he had emerged the victor. Had he failed, his authority as sheriff would have been at an end, though that would probably have been the least of his troubles.

Slowly, uncertainly, the others from Moon Star came up, and he left Crowley to their ministrations, walking across to the lead wagon of the evicted homesteaders. Laurie Martin's sunbonnet had been tipped back, and only her eyes looked alive in a bloodless face. Two or three of the guards from Moon Star stood by uncertainly.

"Since it's getting late, you folks will want to spend the night in town," Boone observed. It was difficult to be matter-of-fact, to speak plainly through bruised and puffy lips. "You can start back to your homesteads tomorrow."

Emhurst came plodding up from the third wagon. His hands had a look of being fitted to a plow, and his eyes still refused to accept what they had just witnessed.

"Start back?" he repeated. "What's there to go back to?"

Boone viewed him in surprise. It was for them he'd been fighting more than anything else. Somehow the answer seemed obvious.

"Why, your land, of course," he said. "Your homes."

"Homes?" Emhurst parroted again. "What homes? They've gone up in smoke. There's nothing left."

"The land is there," Boone reminded. "It's what you came for in the first place, and a year nearer to belonging to you. If you don't want it, of course, that's up to you. As for the buildings—"

His gaze, roving over the uncertain crowd, caught sight of Overcash, a gangly man marked by a restless energy. The long, squat lumber mill, barely visible a mile beyond the town, was his. Overcash had seen the need and the opportunity, and had brought in a saw a couple of years before. The big blade and other necessary equipment had had to be ordered from the East, shipped by steamboat as far as Fort Benton, then laboriously transported overland and set up. Singing River itself had been harnessed to supply motive power.

Timber was available only a few miles to the north, and with the mill in operation, Overcash had been kept busy. The original homestead shacks had been built from some of his boards. A couple of houses in town showed a contrast with the older buildings, made of logs or of rough-hewed lumber.

"You can get lumber from Overcash as soon as you're ready. There will be time enough to rebuild before the cold weather sets in."

"Time, maybe, but what else?" Emhurst countered bitterly. "Who's going to pay for the lumber. We're wiped out, broke."

"Get what lumber and supplies you need," Boone instructed. "Send the bill to Jeb Crowley."

They looked at him unbelievingly, apparently not quite sure if it was he or they who were crazy. Crowley stirred with returning consciousness.

"Where do you get the idea he'd pay for stuff for us?" Emhurst demanded. "You forgettin' that he had us burnt out in the first place?"

"That's what I mean." Boone looked about at the group of the dispossessed. "It was his crew who evicted you, then burnt your buildings? You can swear to that?"

"I can swear a darn sight more'n that, if I let myself go," Emhurst grounted. But Martin, understanding what Boone had in mind, nodded. "We can all testify to that," he said.

"That's all that's necessary. Overcash, let them have what they require; then turn the bill in to Crowley. Should he refuse to pay, we'll put it up to a United States marshal to take action."

Overcash stood hesitant, then nodded slowly. He was a man of vision and ambition. An hour before, it had looked as though any set of homesteaders would be a poor risk for years to come, but now he had a notion that more and more of them would be coming, a tide which nothing could stem. In his business, it paid to be on the side of the most customers.

"I'll chance letting them have the lumber," he agreed.

Emhurst wagged his head, torn by doubts. It had seemed that a part of him had died that day as he was compelled to move off the land, forced to watch flames devouring the fruit of his toil, helpless in the face of guns and overwhelming numbers. The prospect had been bleak, since there·was nowhere to go, no real chance to start over. He had already used his homestead rights when filing on this land. Even if a better, safer place could be found elsewhere, abandoned rights could not be transferred.

But there was still a spark of life in him, and now hope fanned it as he looked about at the others and saw their mounting enthusiasm.

"I'd like to go back," he agreed. "We all would. But not if the same thing's going to happen all over again, and once we get a lot more work put in, it'll be wasted."

"What you do is up to you," Boone conceded. He was suddenly very tired, aching and bone-weary, and he wondered fuzzily how he'd gotten into this in the first place. None of it had been of his planning or seeking, yet here he was.

"The law's on your side, as long as you keep the

law in return," he added. "I hope that's good enough. It's all I can say."

"It wasn't good enough this morning—" Emhurst began, but Laurie Martin, who had been watching and listening with returning color, interrupted. She had the look of one who had beheld a vision.

"It's good enough, Mr. Sarsfield—with you to back it," she assured him. "Mr. Emhurst seems to forget that you have just now become sheriff, and that the law has already made a great change. We are most grateful to you."

Paul Martin eyed his wife proudly. He had a sense of events, but was inarticulate when it came to getting out the proper words. Laurie not only had the feeling, but she could also supply the words.

"That's right," he agreed. "We'll do our part."

Jeb Crowley stirred, threshing with one arm and a gesture of the head. Except for that pettish gesture. he was subdued by pain, coupled with the realization of defeat. He sat up slowly, his injured limb stretched before him, his eyes wide. There could be no doubt that he had heard and understood. Overcash, always cautious and already regretting the impulse which had led him to speak, looked at him.

"That's all right with you, Mr. Crowley—about sendin' you the bill for the lumber?"

Crowley shrugged angrily, then winced at the thrust of pain from his leg through his body. He hesitated, then added shortly. Always a gambler, he had long since learned how to be a good loser. And this had been a gamble, as he had realized.

That morning there had seemed no question as to his ability to get away with it. Should the nesters turn to the law, Purdy would mouth pious nothings and that was all. Burning the buildings had been merely a capstone to their humiliation.

Conditions had altered, and Sarsfield was right in affirming that the government would not look kindly upon so high-handed a procedure. As long as he backed them, they could get action from a higher authority. It might be better to pay than to have a marshal sent in.

The cost of the lumber did not bother him; it was the humiliation at the hands of his former employee which rankled. And this bill could be added to that score.

"That part is all right," he agreed. "I'll settle it all with you, Sarsfield—soon's I'm able to walk again. It will be my personal pleasure to kill you."

In the words was a double significance. The homesteaders could go ahead without fear of attack as long as Boone Sarsfield was sheriff. All other matters were secondary to Crowley. Not even Pratt Levinger, or the members of the crew, should take any drastic action. Boone was his meat.

That he would seek to make good his threat at the

earliest possible date, Boone had no doubt. Once embarked upon a course, the boss of Moon Star might change his methods but not his purpose. The homesteaders would be assured of safety only until the sheriff had been dealt with.

The next meeting between Sarsfield and himself would be with guns. Crowley intended that it should be final.

Boone offered no comment. The possession of a sheriff's star offered no personal immunity. In some respects it was more like a target, to be used as such.

He was uncertain whether or not most of the homesteaders understood the latent implication of Jeb's position. They did know that Crowley was allowing them to go back, that he would pay for the buildings he had ordered destroyed, and they were lifted out of despondency. They moved to the edge of town to set up camp. Only a few possessions had been salvaged, but this night's stop would not be as cheerless as it had threatened to be an hour before.

To cover his outward appearance of back-tracking, Crowley sharply ordered his men to quit standing around, and to hustle up a team and a wagon, with hay on the bottom of the box.

"Think I want to lay out here all night?" he growled. "Get the wagon and get me home."

He glared angrily as Boone crossed to look down at him, then, heedless of Crowley's scowl, dropped on a knee to examined the injured limb.

"Get away from me," Crowley snarled. "This is no business of yours—not till I can walk on it again, at least!"

"You're proddy as an outcast buffalo, ain't you?" Boone returned. "Don't know that I can blame you too much. . . ." Crowley's face went white as Boone probed with thumb and finger at the break, but he stifled a groan. Boone came to his feet again.

"Appears to be a clean break. You boys forget about that wagon. Get a door instead, and move him inside a house. And one of you head for the next county seat and bring back a doctor, fast as you can manage. No time to waste."

"Darn it, who's giving the orders around here?" Crowley complained. "I say I'm going home—"

"And I say you're not," Boone contradicted. "It would solve a few problems for me, if I let you be stubborn, for such a trip might kill you, tough as you are. You fellows see if Mrs. Parrish will take in such a cranky old coot," he added. "She's about the best nurse around, and he'll need good care."

7

Boone's former crew members scurried about, obeying his orders. They appreciated that something had to be done for Crowley, and neither he nor Pratt Levinger could take charge. Also, like the others who had watched, they were impressed. Boone Sarsfield had been a top hand, though in that position there had been nothing particularly noteworthy in his performance. Now, as sheriff, he was displaying qualities which commanded respect.

"I'd like for a couple of you to come over to the jail and scrub out a cell for Pratt," Boone added. "The place is filthy, and he deserves a decent room in which to spend the night."

They obeyed that order also, because of the way he put it. He was not responsible for the condition the jail had been in; his consideration for Levinger was unusual.

Boone unlocked another cell, found them a bucket and mop, then crossed to the store and asked for a blanket. He dug in his pocket for money, but the proprietor, who had watched the events on the street with absorbed interest, refused to accept pay.

"You getting this for Levinger?" he asked. "In that case, I'll donate it. Looks like you could use a new shirt for yourself, too."

"Why, thanks; maybe I'll get one, soon as I have time," Boone accepted, and trudged back through the gathering darkness. The adjoining cell had been well scrubbed, and he thanked his assistants, then ushered them out at the door and returned to transfer Levinger, tossing him the blanket.

"I'll see that you get some supper," he promised, and went out. The foreman appeared sobered by recent events, and grateful for cleaner quarters.

Boone hesitated, wondering what to do next. The warmth of the afternoon still lingered, and this was usually his favorite time of day, when he relaxed, drinking in deep lungfuls of the soft air and watching the pattern of stars come out. But that was only for those whose work was done.

The day had been eventful, though confusing in some respects. He had a job again, a new respect in the community, and there would be no further challenge to his authority. His clashes, first with Levinger, then with Jeb Crowley, had settled that.

For all that, he lacked a room or any place to stay, and he was desperately tired, more shaken from the batering of Crowley's fists than he cared to admit.

The fight could just as easily have gone the other way, in which event he'd have been discredited, finished in that part of the country. That would have been unbearable, after he had intervened in behalf of the homesteaders, with Helen Hankinson backing him so strongly.

As though she had been conjured up by his thoughts, the girl spoke from beside him.

"You've made a wonderful beginning," she commended him, "better than anyone else thought you could, I'm sure. But you're all done in, and no wonder. Come along with me."

Her voice was wonderfully gentle, yet it held an unmistakable note of pride. Her words implied that she had had no doubts as to the outcome. He fell into step automatically, then paused.

"I guess I am sort of beat," he acknowledged. "And I haven't had a chance to thank you for intervenin' on my side—when I sure needed it. But I'll have to find a room—"

"I know," she agreed. "I'm staying at Ma Jackson's, and she has another room for rent. I'm sure she'll be glad to have you for a roomer."

Too tired to think, he submitted gratefully. He knew Ma Jackson by reputation as a forthright character who exerted a strong influence on the community. At one time she had been the schoolteacher, and now, a widow, she remained more or less an instructor at large.

She opened the door at Helen's knock, peering from under a piled-up bun of still black hair, in which a high comb sparkled from the reflection of the lamp on the kitchen table.

"I brought the sheriff to take your extra room, Ma," Helen explained. "He needs a place to stay."

"You did just right," Ma agreed, her eyes swift but sympathetic as they ranged over his face and torn shirt. "My land, you're really battered, which, considering the fracas you were in, is not to be wondered at. Sit down in this rocker and let me do a few things to your face."

His protests overruled, Boone submitted gratefully. It was pleasant to be fussed over and ministered to by a couple of women, both of whom were wonderfully gentle. Dried blood was washed away, ointment applied, and a deep cut of which he hadn't even been aware was bandaged. As she worked, Ma Jackson talked.

"Nobody supposed that Moon Star could be licked," she observed. "So you gave a double demonstration—and a convincing one! Which they deserved! But I must say that I'm sore disappointed in Jeb Crowley. I thought that he was getting some sense in that hard head of his; at his age it's about time!"

"Is he really as terrible as he sounds?" Helen asked.

"He'd have everyone believe he's worse," Ma snapped. "It's a matter of pride with him—false pride, which to him is a worse burden than the old man of the sea. Pride!" she snorted wrathfully. "Why should the spirit of mortal be proud?"

She bustled away, returning with a shirt which had once belonged to her husband. It was a size too small, but Boone struggled into it. He was conscious of the troubled look in Helen's eyes, of her silence, as though she brooded in secret. He wondered if it was concern for her brother that worried her.

At Mrs. Jackson's suggestion, she brought a bowl of soup and tried to spoon it to him, but, rousing, Boone insisted on sitting at the table and eating. Then, stumbling off to bed, he was instantly asleep.... .

On awakening, he was momentarily puzzled as to where he was and strove to remember. Then memory came back, and his guilty realization that he had overslept dissipated. The sun which came in at a curtained window was high, by which he judged that it must be the middle of the forenoon. Not in years had he slept so late. But now he was his own boss, and after so full a day, there seemed to be justification for his laziness.

Pulling on his boots, he found his muscles creaking with stiffness. Crowley would be just as badly off, not counting his broken leg. Boone found no pleasure in the reflection. Jeb had been his employer too long, a man he'd respected and counted as a friend. The sole good point was that Crowley's mishap removed any immediate necessity of another showdown. Having made his threat, Crowley would do his best to kill Boone as soon as he could walk again.

Ma Jackson was in the kitchen, transforming rumpled linen to crisp order with deft strokes of an iron. She eyed him appraisingly, then nodded approval.

"I've seen men look worse on the morning after, and for a lot less reason," she observed. "I'd offer you breakfast, and glad to, but I have a notion that Helen will be looking for you to eat where she works, I wouldn't want to deprive you of her company. She went to work hours ago."

"Then I'll get on over there," Boone agreed, reflecting with sudden dismay that he'd promised Pratt Levinger to bring him some supper, then had forgotten all about it. By now Pratt must be half-starved, and he'd be in a justifiably bad mood.

Nonetheless, it was a good day to be alive in. The summer had been hot, but now the mornings were cool, and the sun had not entirely dispelled all the bite from the air. Meadow larks wheeled in an adjoining field, flocking in preparation for the journey south, scattering left-over song with prodigal recklessness. Blackbirds in even greater numbers flashed in the sun.

Once again The Red Rooster was empty of customers. Helen studied him anxiously as he came to the counter and leaned his weight on it without sliding onto a stool.

"Good morning," she greeted him. Then, suddenly shy, "I hope you're feeling better."

"I'm fine," he assured her, and managed a convincing grin despite bruised lips. "And sharp-set in the bargain."

"How about hot cakes, ham and coffee? They won't take long to fix."

"That sounds fine. But will you fix some to take out first? Make it a double order. I promised Pratt Levinger to bring him some supper; then, when you ladies got to fussing over me, I was so comfortable and selfish that I forgot all about him."

"He didn't suffer. One of his own men took him a good meal last evening."

Though relieved at the news, Boone carried the tray across before getting his own breakfast. The door to the office was unlocked, also the one leading to the cells, though they were still secure. He reflected that he'd been careless in this matter, that one or two determined men might easily have freed the prisoner. Nothing of the sort had been attempted.

Pratt hungrily accepted the tray.

"Slim had to hand stuff in through the bars for my

supper," he observed. "But after what happened, I'm not complaining. How's Crowley today?"

"I haven't heard," Boone confessed. "I just got up. Sort of overslept."

"I'll say you did." Levinger studied him soberly in the light from an adjoining window. "I can't blame you. But do I have to stay shut up here? There's work to be done."

"I'll keep it in mind," Boone promised, and returned to his own breakfast. Helen watched him eat, bringing a fresh stack of hot cakes and keeping his coffee cup filled. He thought he understood her solicitude. She had helped persuade him to take the job, and it had kicked back with a vengeance, so no doubt she felt responsible.

"Your brother's out of town?" he asked.

"Yes." She did not amplify, but it seemed to Boone that the subject of Bob was not overly pleasant. If he'd settle down and work the way she did—but the boy was young, of course. And a restless, reckless boy could stumble into a lot of trouble.

"You worked for Jeb Crowley for quite a while, didn't you?" she asked.

"Several years." Boone nodded. "Up till yesterday."

"Then I'm surprised that he'd treat you as he did."

"He wanted me to run the homesteaders off. He figured they were butcherin' his calves to get something to eat—and maybe they were. I didn't know, and I was willing to give them the benefit of the doubt. Donovan sort of planted the idea, and he listens to Donovan."

"Is he a good influence—Donovan, I mean?"

"I've wondered," Boone confessed. "Anyway, he's always been Jeb's best friend—or he's made Jeb believe he was. After I quit, then turned up here to interfere with what Crowley was doing—it rawed him, of course. He can't stand being crossed."

Boone was still wondering when he recrossed the street to the jail. There were a lot of answers which he'd have liked to have, and he had a feeling that it was the same with Helen Hankinson. But there were also a lot of questions difficult to bring into the open.

He unlocked the cell door and motioned toward the outer air as Levinger stood up uncertainly.

"Do you mean you're letting me go?" he asked.

"Crowley's flat on his back for a while. Somebody's got to look after the ranch."

Pratt hesitated, clearly of a mind to make some remark, then shook his head and stalked away in silence.

A strange team of sorrel trotting horses stood with a buggy in front of Mrs. Parrish's house. Then the doctor emerged, carrying a black bag. He nodded tiredly when Boone spoke.

"He'll do." He shrugged. "The leg was badly swollen, and it was difficult to set the bone properly, but I managed. He'll have to keep off it awhile—which will probably be the hardest part of the whole affair, for him."

"Well, at least he hasn't been forgotten by his neighbors," Boone observed. "He'll have company."

"Right now he'd be better off without any," the doctor grunted, climbed into his own buggy and shook the reins. "But I guess he's tough enough to take it."

Another buggy was pulling up as the doctor drove out of town. Having noticed the coal-black team, Boone had no need to ask questions. Rusty Donovan had come to call.

8.

Donovan had changed his mind the day before, remaining on the outskirts of town when he learned what had happened, then returning to Catclaw. Crowley would be in no shape for company at the moment.

Today, however, he was back, as casually as if a seventy-mile round trip were of no consequence, drawing off his gloves as he entered the sick room, staring accusingly down at the man on the bed. His voice boomed through the house.

"What's the world coming to?" he demanded. "Here it's noon, and you still in bed! I never thought I'd live to see the day."

If he was working for a chuckle, he failed. Crowley grunted. His face was still white from the pain of having had the bone set and splinted.

"Ain't it bad enough to be pawed over by a horse-doctor, without a man havin' to listen to the brayin' of a jackass on top of that?" he asked.

Donovan grinned, helping himself to a chair. "As long as you're mad, you're all right," he said comfortably. "I met the nesters on their way back as I came in. A couple of them had their wagons piled high with lumber."

"I guess you've heard how it happened. Seemed like it might be the best way to handle it."

"Too bad you'd fired Sarsfield," Donovan sympathized. "He'd have stayed loyal if he'd been taking your pay."

"How loyal did he stay while he *was* takin' my pay?" Crowley snarled. "But let him strut. His day will come."

"Sure, sure. If there's anything I can do to help, Jeb—while you're sort of kept from looking after certain chores yourself—"

"I'll kill my own rattlesnakes," Crowley assured him venomously. "Delayin' the day will just make the job that much sweeter when the time comes!"

Boone spent the afternoon cleaning up the cell block, then making a start on the office. The one cell had been scrubbed, but the place as a whole was filthy. Open doors and windows gave the air its first complete freshening, he assumed, since his predecessor had been in charge. He burned mattresses and blankets, replacing them with new ones and charging these to the county. He wasn't sure if there were any funds for such a purpose, but went on the assumption that there should be.

It was a relief when the place was finally clean, the cot in the office so tempting that he eyed it wistfully. Regretfully he turned away. A man could sleep when there was nothing else to be done. Right now, unless he has very much mistaken, there was a lot which clamored for his attention.

When he had been on hands and knees with a bucket and scrub brush, his mind had kept busy. Much had happened since he'd left the train and climbed on the overloaded stage, with his own bag and ten thousand dollars of Jeb Crowley's money in it; money which he had come very near to losing.

It might have been chance or coincidence that the robbery attempt had been made, but there were too many complicating factors for him to accept such a conclusion. For instance, he'd paid over the money for the herd of yearlings, accordings to Crowley's instructions, before returning to Singing River and Moon Star.

A part of the crew from Moon Star had been on hand to bring back the herd. By rights, they should have arrived at Singing River the day before, or at least by today.

So far there had been no sign of them.

He was no longer in Crowley's employ, and after what had happened, he could hardly be said to be in Crowley's debt. Nonetheless, he felt a sense of responsibility. He'd bought the herd, and however inadvertently, he'd messed up the normal routine at Moon Star. Crowley was unable to move, too sick to give proper attention to such matters. Pratt Levinger might get around to it in a day or so—but an extra day or so might be too long a delay. There had to be a reason for the herd failing to arrive. Coupling this with other recent happenings, some of them trivial at least on the surface, he had a grim suspicion as to what that might be.

All other reasons aside, he was sheriff, and as such he had a responsibility.

It would be pleasant to talk things over with Helen Hankinson, to spend another night resting. But neither course would be expedient. The thought was as unpleasant as the prospect of a long ride ahead, but some chores couldn't be put off. Boone got a horse and rode out silently, in the deepening night.

Donovan was smiling as he walked down the street, with an expression which seemed to indicate that, from his point of view, all was well with the world. If Crowley had appreciated the gesture of driving all the way in to town to see him, he had given no indication of it, but Donovan had not looked for any word of thanks.

From across the street, standing on the steps of the post office, Zeke Farley hailed him, then motioned for him to come across. Normally, Donovan left such chores as picking up the mail to some of his men. Now, however, he responded to the summons.

"Thought you might want to know about this," the postmaster explained. "There's a letter here for you. Just come in. Marked special delivery, whatever in tarnation that means." He shook his head over it. "All the years I've handled the mail here, this is the first time I ever got one of that sort."

"First time I've ever gotten one like that, either," Donovan confessed. He examined the envelope with a mounting excitement, then ripped it open and spread out the page. A second time he read the message, more slowly, before folding the sheet and tucking it back in the envelope. Zeke watched with bright-eyed interest.

"Somethin' important, maybe?" he suggested.

"Might be," Donovan admitted. Disregarding Farley's unsatisfied curiosity, he returned to the street.

He was thoughtful now, though his good humor was in no way diminished. He had been about to get his team and drive out, to return to Catclaw. Instead, he angled across to The Red Rooster, climbing on a stool and ordering a cup of coffee and a piece of pie. Such an action was unheard of for him at that hour of the day, but it afforded him an opportunity to meet and study the girl who waited on him.

What he saw pleased him. His glance kindled at sight of Helen, and for a moment a strange, inscrutable expression came in to his eyes.

"That's good coffee," he observed. "I'd like another cup. . . . Good pie, too. Best I ever ate here in town. You make it?"

Helen's reply was brief. "Yes."

"Takes a real cook to make good pie. Ain't many can manage. Mostly the crust's either too tough or too soggy, or it'll be burnt on the bottom and raw in the middle. . . . You're new here in town, ain't you?"

"I just came a few days ago," she acknowledged.

"That accounts for it. The word 'll get around." He grinned, wiping his mouth with the back of a hand. "Maybe I'd better put in my oar *before* it gets known just how good a cook you are. You wouldn't be interested in cookin' for a ranch crew, now?"

Helen checked the prompt negative which came to her lips. She had recognized him as soon as he entered, not alone from a prior description of the other big rancher, but from the air of proprietorship which was an arrogant if unconscious part of him. Her eyes narrowed.

"What crew would that be?" she countered.

Donovan looked surprised. "Why, the Catclaw," he said. "My outfit. I'm Rusty Donovan. And we sure could use some good cooking for a change." Warming to his subject, he pursued it eagerly. "I don't know what you're makin' here, though, knowin' your employer, I can guess that he don't pay any more'n he has to. At the ranch, it would be fifty a month and found."

Since found would include room and board, it would be twice as good a deal as she received at The Red Rooster. Donovan pursued the subject.

"You must be Helen Hankinson," he added. "Now I stop to think of it, I've heard you mentioned."

"Yes, that's my name," Helen admitted. She filled his cup again.

"Mighty pretty name—Helen," Donovan observed. "How about it? You wouldn't have to work any harder on Catclaw than you do here. Maybe not so hard. You'd be given an assistant—somebody to peel spuds, wash dishes and that sort of thing."

Helen hesitated. The offer was more tempting than perhaps he realized. On the other hand, there were impelling reasons to remain where she was. Some of these she was not ready to admit even to herself; still, she was conscious of them. Others were clear enough.

Donovan looked at her expectantly. "How about it?" he persisted. "You going to take pity on the misused stomachs of a hungry crew and give us some fittin' fodder for a change?"

Helen laughed, but shook her head.

"You don't know whether I can cook anything except a pie or not," she reminded him. "I might turn out to be the world's worst cook, with everything else—"

Donovan shook his head vigorously, the enthusiasm in his eyes and his voice increasing.

"I sure wouldn't buy that. Anyhow, if I'm willing to take a chance, you could do as much."

"I'd have to think it over," she returned. "Even if I should decide to accept, I couldn't walk out without giving notice."

"Well, think it over, then. I'll drop around next time I'm in town." At the door, he looked back. "Catclaw's the biggest, best ranch in this country. You'd like it."

9.

Riding, Boone found much to think about. Half-consciously his senses noted the passing show—the sharp fragrance of smartweed from the rim of a deep pool of the creek, the splash of a muskrat as his horse passed on the road. A rabbit made a gray shadow, and the bright eyes of a night prowler stared from a thicket.

For a time he allowed his thoughts to dwell on Helen Hankinson, and the times that she had befriended him, all within a few days. Besides the vague sense of familiarity which she aroused in him, as though he had known her somewhere, there was something out of the ordinary about the Hankinsons, some unanswered questions which might prove intriguing.

He suspected that she might wonder at his failure to return to his room; she might even be worried about him when he failed to show up anywhere in town the next day. Such concern, on the part of so attractive a woman, was not only new in his experience, but pleasant. . . .

Perhaps he was being foolish to take this ride in the first place, when no one had asked him to, and no complaints had been made. Though sheriff, he owed no debt to Moon Star, none to the man who had promised to kill him as soon as he was able.

Yet Jeb Crowley was more easily hoodwinked than he realized or would ever admit. And basically he was a decent man. Those qualities made a difference. And now since Crowley was flat on his back, this matter was Boone's responsibility if not his fault.

A half-moon prowled the night sky, affording ample light. The miles fell behind; the land was wide and empty. It was that emptiness which disturbed him; there was no sign of the herd anywhere along the way.

Such tardiness on the trail spelled trouble. The only question was the nature which it might take.

He was bone-weary, ready when the moon slid below the horizon to snatch a few hours of sleep. But as it vanished, another light glimmered far to the side, this one low and man-made. Boone studied it, surprised. Any sort of a light was rare at that hour, even in a town. Almost always they were out by midnight.

Off there the nearest approach to a town was a saloon, isolated in lonely grandeur miles from any other habitation. Despite its location, Louie's place enjoyed good patronage, being somewhat in the nature of an oasis. Meals were served as well as liquid refreshment.

Boone had never seen the saloon, but the light must come from it. The oddity was that Louie's should still be open at this hour.

A coulee commenced at one side, meandering away in a long, brush-lined gash through otherwise untrammeled plain. Near its head stood a log house, then the saloon. On either side of the saloon were set hitch-rails for the accommodation of visitors' horses. The rail at the far side was vacant, but several horses lined the nearer one, standing despondently, with droping heads. That, too, was highly unusual: that saddled animals should be tied at such a place at so late an hour.

Familiar with the remuda on Moon Star as he was, Boone did not need a look at the brands to be certain that these horses belonged to the big ranch.

Dismounting, he approached, choosing an uncurtained window in preference to the door. A single lamp was suspended from the ceiling near the middle of the room, leaving the edges in shadow. At first glance, it appeared that all the occupants of the room must be asleep, but that was an illusion. Some were asleep, but others were awake, though barely.

Two men sat at a table, owlishly engaged in a game of cards. Their motions were so slow as to seem mechanical, but they were resisting the impulse to give in to sleep. Boone recognized their condition, a state to which too much liquor brought some drinkers at a certain stage.

A bartender nodded frankly in a chair behind the bar, and others in the room were openly slumbering, stretched on the floor or lolling in chairs.

It was an unusual spectacle, not the least surprising part being that the saloon should be kept open all night, after all customers were long past any inclination to buy. Normally, they would have been shoved out hours before, at the usual closing time.

Boone counted, with surprise. The entire crew which had been sent to drive back the newly purchased herd was there. There was no sign of the cattle, and that meant that no one had been left to look after them.

Crossing to the cabin, Boone knocked on the door. It required some sharp rapping before he elicited any response. Then Big Louie, blinking and plainly annoyed, opened the door and peered out. He wore long red underwear, and his bare feet protruded on the rough board floor.

"What you want?" he growled. "What's the idea, wakin' a man at this time o' night?" He squinted at the light still showing in the saloon. "If you want a drink, go over there. The bar's open."

"That's what I wanted to ask you about," Boone informed him. "What's the reason for keeping your saloon open, long past the usual hour?"

Louie scowled. "Judgin' from the horses, there's still customers. So if you want somethin', go there, 'stead of botherin' me—"

He sought unsuccessfully to shut the door, but

found a boot in the way. Boone's next question shocked him wide awake.

"You've got Moon Star men in there—drunk or doped, likely both. A crew who are supposed to be looking after a herd of cattle. Maybe you can guess what Jeb Crowley will do to you if that bunch is lost!"

Big Louie blinked uncertainly, then swallowed. His Adam's apple seemed to catch and stick in his throat before he could bring it under control.

"Uh—Crowley?" he repeated. "What—who are you?"

"I used to work for Crowley," Boone informed him. "Right now, I'm the sheriff of this county." He indicated the star on his shirt, and Louie goggled at it. "It strikes me that some mighty funny shenanigans are going on, and whatever it is, you're right in the middle. If Crowley's herd is lost, while you keep his men drunk and off their jobs, then I'd hate to be in your boots once he finds out about it."

"A herd, did you say?" Louie repeated. "I didn't know they was supposed to be lookin' after no herd," he added, but the words lacked conviction.

"You know it now," Boone pointed out. "You'd better get them awake and sobered up to the point where they can ride, and do it soon. Otherwise, when the next crew from Moon Star show up, they'll come with guns and a torch."

Louie by now was thoroughly frightened. There was no doubt in Boone's mind that he must have been fully aware of the circumstances from the first, and might even be involved in the steal, though indirectly. The crew must have been there for a couple of days. They were so sodenly drunk that they had lost all sense of time or responsibilty.

To pretend that he had merely sold liquor to customers as they appeared was one thing; to be caught with a crew in this condition, at this hour of the morning, was entirely different, and Louie knew it. For the sheriff to be the witness was the worst possible climax to the episode.

Normally, once the delinquent crew sobered enough to realize what they had done and, much worse, what they had failed to do, they would be overcome by a sense of guilt. Harried by fear, they would voice no complaints regarding the saloon or its hospitality. They would be too busy making their way out of the country by the most direct route, anxious to put as much distance as possible between themselves and their former employer.

The bar was a long way from Moon Star and its range, isolated, perfect for such a trick as was being played on the crew. Knowing the men, Boone could guess how it had been worked. Tired and bored with driving the cattle, someone had invited them to swing past the saloon and wash the dust of the trail from their throats. Undoubtedly they had planned on only a single drink.

But one drink had been followed by many more, which indicated that skulduggery had been practiced. While they forgot duty, the herd had disappeared.

"I sure didn't know nothin' about a herd," Louie proclaimed self-righteously. "If I had, I'd have sent them on their way, hours ago. I'll be right over there, soon's I can get some clothes on."

Under the circumstances, that was the best that could be hoped for. Louie was as good as his word. He came promptly, opening and closing the door of the saloon with a bang which disturbed the somnolent men, shouting to the bartender to bestir himself, then moving about to rouse the sleepers. That was far from easy, confirming Boone's hunch that some of the drinks had been doped. Still stupefied, the men slowly returned to awareness, blinking in the increased light as all the lamps were lit. There were seven in all.

"Boil a pot of coffee," Louie instructed the bartender. "Make it strong. Why, blast it, these fellows are supposed to be lookin' after a herd of cattle. I sure wisht I'd known that, but when they showed up here without the critters, how'd you and me guess? But we got to get them on their feet and ridin', quick as we can."

His willingness to cooperate was disturbing, indicating as it did that by now the stolen herd must be so far away that he had little fear that they could be found or overtaken.

The men drank the hot coffee, gradually sobering, moaning as they nursed aching heads, bothered still more by the realization of how remiss they had been in their duty, and the consequences should the herd be lost. They eyed Boone and the badge of his office uncertainly, while he brought them up to date on recent history.

"Crowley's in town with a broken leg," he explained. "But that won't stop him from sending Levinger after you—unless you find that herd again and deliver it, in good shape."

They gleared balefully at Louie as they began to realize the full extent of the calamity, but Boone's hope that they might voice revealing charges against him was not realized. Apparently the conspirators had been too clever for that. They had no proof that he had done anything more than sell them the drinks they asked for. As a further proof of his good intentions, he served breakfast to everyone without charge.

By that time, dawn was across the land, showing it to be wide and empty. Boone lingered as the others swung into saddles.

"Likely we can find the trail and track the cattle by the sign along the trail," he observed. "But a short cut might save us a lot of riding, if we knew which way to go." He looked down at Louie, allowing the words to sink in. "If the boys show up with the herd in good shape, Crowley'll probably overlook some of the mistakes that have been made. But if they don't —then you can guess what you can expect from him!"

Big Louie swallowed again, as uncomfortably as before. Such a warning, spoken by the sheriff, had an ominous sound.

"I wouldn't know a thing abont what might have happened to their herd while those boys was havin' themselves a time here," he protested. "But I do know this country pretty well, and there's somethin' in what you say. Was I tryin' to get away with a bunch—like you seem to think might be the case here—why, I'd figure that the likeliest way would be just to swing straight north. 'Course, there's a lot of rough country farther west that a herd could be lost or hid in. But the border's not too far off, in a straight line."

"That's an idea," Boone agreed. "One other thing. Who put you up to doping their whiskey in the first place?"

Louie looked hurt. "Dopin' it? Sheriff, you don't think I'd do a thing like that—"

"I know darn well that you did," Boone informed him. "You lied when you said you hadn't seen the cattle. Look at the droppings around the place here. They're still fairly fresh, and the number indicates a big herd."

Louie goggled again, having overlooked that evidence, or else having supposed that the sheriff would overlook it.

"I—some of the ranchers' stock drift this way every now and then—"

"That won't wash. Another lie, and I'll turn you over to those fellows to handle. *Who put you up to doping that whiskey?*"

Big Louie might be a willing accomplice to crime, but he was hardly of the stuff of which outlaws are made. He understood the sheriff's threat—that the angry crew, brooding now on their troubles, would be allowed to do with him as they pleased. That would mean doing a dance at rope's end.

"I—I—" The wheeze was scarcely above a whisper. "All right, I'll come clean—though I never meant no harm." A crafty light gleamed under bushy brows. "I never saw the feller before, but he give me a song an' dance about this same crew bein' mad at him, said they'd string him up if they caught him. Would I put just a leetle stuff in their drinks, to delay 'em long enough so he could get out of their way?

"Well, mister, he was just a kid, and sure scairt. I didn't know nothin' about a herd—I figured they was mebby a posse, and fell for it. That's all."

Boone felt cold as he described, in accurate detail, the man who had persuaded him to do the mischief. It was a perfect picture of Bob Hankinson.

10.

Spurring to catch up with the others, Boone had the feeling that he had been kicked. That the news was not really unexpected made it worse.

For the moment, recovery of the stolen herd came ahead of everything else. The crew, wide awake now and sobered by the realization of what had happened, were following the sign, which led west by north.

Big Louie had actually told him nothing about them which he had not known, but his suggestion might be a clue. An extra day could easily be wasted, following the sign as it led now westward.

"Let's swing north," he suggested. "We've nothing to lose."

The others agreed readily. He was, or had been, one of them, and they assumed that he had taken the job as sheriff with Crowley's full approval. In any case, he was working to save them from a situation which could easily become desperate.

Troubled in mind as they were, still none of them

was inclined to confide in him. Whatever excuse they might give would still amount to self-condemnation. They had allowed themselves to be lured away from duty, and the consequences were still so potentially disastrous that they were shivering in their boots.

Though half-asleep in the saddle, he was sufficiently alert to notice, after riding for a couple of hours, that there was again sign of a good-sized herd. Here the indications were fresher than they had been back at the saloon.

Anxious to hedge his bets, it appeared that Louie had given him a good steer. He might be cut in for a small share of the profits should the stolen herd be gotten safely over the border, but the prospect of Jeb Crowley's vengeance if that happened was even less to his liking.

After a night of riding, Boone found it hard to keep on, but he had to see this through. The fact that he'd have preferred to drop it, for personal reasons, only made his duty more imperative.

If they recovered the herd, Crowley would probably be grateful, but not to the extent of changing his announced intention of killing the sheriff, once he was able to walk again. Crowley liked to boast that he never allowed sentiment to interfere with business.

The sun was warm, the day almost perfect. Bidding the others keep on, Boone stretched on the ground and slept. His horse as well as himself had to have some rest, so the time would not be wasted.

When he aroused, the sun was declining. Boone ate the lunch which Louie had provided for each man, then went on. The rest had done both himself and his horse a lot of good.

The sign was increasingly fresh, but there was still no glimpse of the cattle, who were unquestionably being hurried in an effort to get them over the border. That invisible line could not be very far away. Boone was sure that its somewhat mythical presence would not stop the others from Moon Star, certainly not if they caught sight of the herd. In that case, he'd probably follow also. Such action on the part of a sheriff might be questionable, but actually the line wouldn't make much difference—unless they encountered a Mountie. But that possibility was remote.

The sun was setting when he heard the boom of guns, still to the north. There was nothing to indicate whether the boundary between nations might be nearby or not. Markers were few and far apart, usually unnoticed except by men who knew their locations. Which perhaps was just as well, for he suspected that they might already be into Canada.

The country was the same—wide open prairie, broken by an occasional coulee, lifts of rimrock, low hills, scattered clumps of brush or trees. Streams were infrequent, but the sea of grass stretched on every hand. Undoubtedly this land was claimed by some cattle outfit, but there had been no sign of human occupancy for hours.

All at once, the sun was gone and dusk was across the land, like a drawn curtain. The guns had ceased to growl, after a period of angry mutterings. Then he heard a new sound, unmistakable to trained ears—the noise of a big herd on the move.

He saw it then, spread out, tired animals moving reluctantly, urged on by the voices of his former companions. One gave a shout of recognition.

"We got 'em, Boone! Caught up with three or four fellers, half dead on their feet and almost asleep. They scattered in a hurry when we busted out at them, shooting!"

That was encouraging, and the others were in high spirits now that the lost herd had been recovered. There might still be explanations required, but if they showed up with the herd intact, that would go a long way toward appeasing their employer.

"We kind of wanted to keep going till you caught up, but now that you're here, what say we camp for the night? We're plenty tired, and these yearlings are near dead on their feet."

"Better keep going awhile longer," Boone demurred, "just in case—"

As though his own suggestion might not be sufficiently convincing, a gun crashed sharply from the side, answered by another from the opposite edge of the herd. There came a rush of hoofs; then riders swept at them in a sudden savage counter-attack.

The next few minutes were as hectic as they were confusing. Surprised but unhurt by the assault of Moon Star's men, the rustlers had withdrawn, then taken stock and regrouped. Now they were attempting a recovery.

In the darkness, the guns were ineffectual, more a gesture than dangerous. But it appeared that at least a few additions had been made to the opposing ranks.

The attackers' greatest handicap was the reluctance of the cattle to respond to any sort of excitement or persuasion. For at least a couple of days they had been hurried at top speed toward the border, covering nearly twice as many miles as they would normally travel under such conditions. They were overtired, at the limit of endurance, and at such times cattle grew stubborn, scarcely responding to any sort of attempt to force them along.

The rush of the outlaws to swing them met with failure. They stood staring stupidly. Boone took charge, shouting for his companions to group up behind him. Once that was done, they sought out the enemy; and then the guns, at close range, spoke to grim purpose.

Boone felt the pluck of lead through the crown of his hat, twitching it about. He fired at the flash, and a yell indicated that he'd scored at least as close a hit. All at once the ghostly ranks broke, swinging into hasty retreat.

One figure was at the side, hampered by a nervous cayuse which clearly disliked gunfire, bucking and sunfishing. Boone swung fast, and his sudden growl set the other horse to renewed plunging.

"Lift 'em, mister! I'm taking you in!"

He felt a sense of grim elation. Here, at last, was a prisoner, and a frightened man might be persuaded to talk. There were a lot of answers he was anxious to receive.

Then, as he edged his horse alongside, peering at the other man in the half-light, shock mingled with dismay. Despite the information which Big Louie had given him, this was the last man he'd expected to find or wanted to see. Now it was too late for a change of mind, since the others were coming up. His prisoner was Bob Hankinson.

11.

Tired as the cattle were, it was necessary to let them stop where they were. Most of the herd immediately dropped to the ground and stretched out, giving the appearance of dead animals. Anger built in Boone at the sight. It was senseless cruelty to push stock in such fashion, and they would be slow in recovering. The inviolate rule of a good cattleman was that a herd must always be allowed to pick its own pace, never be hurried.

There was no outlet for his anger there, since it was the rustlers who had been responsible, and the only one of those taken captive had been Bob Hankinson. Sarsfield studied him morosely. Hankinson had offered no resistance, nor did he volunteer any explanation for his presence at such a time and place. He was cheerful, helpful in every way possible. It was as though he did not realize his own predicament or the one in which he had placed the sheriff.

The aroma of bacon and coffee stirred Boone to

wakefulness. Air and ground alike were frosty, and his glance went automatically to the blanket a few feet away where Hankinson had slept. He was guiltily relieved to see that it was empty, but the feeling was short-lived as he turned the other way. It was Bob who hunkered over the cook fire, carefully tending the pan of bacon. He grinned as he caught Boone's glance.

"Thought I'd better fix some breakfast. About the least I can do. I'm likely not quite so tired as the rest of you."

Some of the cattle were beginning to stir also, starting to crop the grass. There had been no alarms or farther interruptions during the night.

He had carefully refrained from tying Hankinson, or setting a guard. It would have been easy for Bob to decamp during the night. In addition, it was his supplies from which their breakfast came.

The cattle were famished, having been allowed scant time for grazing, and the tiredness of overexertion slowed them also. They made no more than five miles that day, less than half the usual distance. By the following one, they were able to push ahead at a reasonable pace.

Boone considered going on with Bob, getting back to Singing River and his job, and leaving the crew to bring the cattle. The herd was their responsibility, not his. But he dreaded the return, and the herd afforded a reasonable excuse for delaying it as long as possible.

Pratt Levinger and Slim met them the next day, Levinger having become uneasy at the failure of the herd to arrive. He stared somberly at sight of Boone, but the truculence of former days was gone from his voice.

"I halfway expected to find you when I found them," he confessed, "providin' I found them at all. What happened?"

"The boys ran into a little trouble." Boone waved a hand. "Ask them."

Levinger listened in silence, while the others gave a factual account of their folly, allowing full credit for what Boone had done. At the end, his shrug was weary.

"I knew something was wrong," he acknowledged. "Looks like Moon Star—and me in particular—owe a lot to you, Boone. The herd would have been lost if you hadn't taken a hand. And there'd have been the devil to pay then, for sure." He brooded a moment, shaking his head.

"I can't figure this out," he confessed. "If trouble had started *after* Crowley was flat on his back, it would make sense. But this scheme to steal the herd must have been planned and well along before you two tangled. And I didn't believe that anyone would risk pickin' on Moon Star!"

That was the crux of the situation, the question which nagged at Boone as well. This sort of thing was new, and he doubted if stealing the herd was an isolated incident. Change was in the wind; here was something big, and potentially explosive.

"Are you still sticking along with the herd, Boone?" Levinger asked. "Maybe you're anxious to get back to town. If you are, go ahead. But if you ain't—I ought to be at the ranch. I've sort of a hunch—" He made an encompassing gesture with both hands, and allowed it to go at that. Boone nodded.

"Likely you're right. I'll stay with the cattle till we reach Singing River. You might leave word as you go through town, so folks will know what's going on."

"I'll do that," Levinger agreed. "Give Crowley a fresh cud to chew on," he added dryly, "one he'll near choke on."

That explanation would save him one when he returned a prospect to which he had looked forward almost with dread. His hopes were scarcely improved when the town was finally sighted. The herd was bedded down a few miles away. Like them, the town was asleep, showing little change from the time when he'd slipped out a week before. Not a light was showing as he let himself into the livery stable, Bob Hankinson at his heels. In silence they stabled and fed their horses.

Bob had followed him into town as a matter of course. There had been no coercion at any time, or any attempt at escape on his part. He had offered no excuses, no explanations.

They returned to the street, where the buildings loomed dark and vaguely unfriendly. Boone was dog-tired, and he knew that his companion must be the same.

"I guess I'll bed down on the bunk in the sheriff's office," he decided. "Save waking folks up in the middle of the night."

"You got a bunk for me, too?" Bob asked. "One of the jail beds should do fine."

"No reason why not, I guess," Boone agreed. He did not bother to light a lamp. Since he'd scrubbed the cells out, the cell doors had stood unlocked and open. "Take your pick."

Hankinson was still asleep when Boone awoke the next morning. The boy looked young and innocent, and the lines of his face reminded Boone sharply of his sister. Without disturbing him, Boone tugged on his boots and went out.

Elisha Peabody came to Singing River at dawn, almost exactly as he had first done two decades before. We stood tall and cadaverous, and the hollows in his cheeks were more pronounced than they had been on that earlier visit, the bony structure of his face now sharply defined. Today, however, a patriarchal beard, its dark brown faintly salted with gray, concealed the austerity, lending him an appearance of dignity.

He dismounted, trying his horse, then stood to look about, his eyes clouding briefly at his memories. He had come there first as a hired mercenary, a trouble-maker, and he was returning after this lapse of years with a similar mission in mind.

After so long a time, no one was likely to recognize him, especially with a beard, and that was well enough. Somehow, he was not entirely proud of his role, but the pay was good, and that was what counted. A man had to make a living, and his talents ran to the nefarious and the devious.

A door opened and closed. Stepping back in to the shelter of an alleyway, Peabody watched as Boone Sarsfield emerged from the sheriff's office, then went past. Having ridden for a day in the stage with him, Peabody had no difficulty recognizing him, despite the week's stubble of beard on his face. It seemed apparent that the sheriff had gotten into town late, then had slept in his office.

No one else was abroad at that house. Cat-footed from long habit, Peabody moved along the street. He let himself into the office, standing a moment to look around. He had no particular objective in mind, and was impelled mostly by curiosity, the possibility that something might turn up. It was surprising how often something did when one looked persistently. A bear, upending stones and rotten logs, found bugs beneath most of them.

The door leading back to the cells was open. Peabody peered into the dim interior of the jail. He made out a man asleep on one of the bunks, observed that the cell door stood open. After a moment, he recognized another fellow-traveler on the stagecoach, and a gleam of hatred lighted the pale eyes, which made such a contrast to the patriarchial dignity of the beard beneath.

Bob Hankinson, by his intervention, had spoiled Peabody's plan to snatch ten thousand dollars in cash, and that was an unforgivable affront. Here was a chance to pay the boy back, at least in some slight degree.

The cells, Peabody observed, locked with padlocks, and this lock was open and in the hasp. Smiling like a small boy playing a trick, Peabody closed the door softly, then snapped the lock shut. The town was still asleep when he came back to the street.

DONOVAN twisted his head to one side, then the other, looking at himself in the mirror of the Hard-luck Mercantile, also the smaller glass which the proprietor held solicitously. He noted approvingly not only the fit of the new suit, but how broad were the shoulders which filled it, slimming to a trim waist.

The years had dealt lightly with him, and there was none of the ungainly, almost sloppy appearance which characterized Jeb Crowley.

"Not bad, Ed," Donovan decided. "Not bad at all. I really needed a new suit, too."

"I'll say you did, Mr. Donovan," Ed McHugh approved. Years before, it had been Ed and Rusty, but he had dropped the familiar first name as Catclaw prospered. "Must be all of five years since you've had a new one. And a man in your position needs good clothes."

"I guess you're right," Donovan conceded. "Maybe I was growing a mite careless, living off on the ranch and alone, the way I do. A man rightly shouldn't be alone. But this takes care of clothes. I'll need a new hat to go with it—a white one, I think."

Presently, jowls blue from the razor and resplendent in his new plumage, he came out to the street, hesitating briefly. No friend could have been more faithful; he made the long ride into town each day to cheer the injured man at Parrish's. If, after each visit with Crowley, he chose to stop for a cup of coffee at The Red Rooster before the ride back to the ranch, there was nothing extraordinary in that, either.

Today he decided to reverse the usual order of events by going first to the restaurant. Crowley had been less appreciative of his visits, acting as snarling and ornery as the bear he resembled as the bone in his leg commenced to knit. Undoubtedly it was painful, and the news of the world, at least the world which he had so long dominated, was scarcely cheering.

Crowley had been worried by the failure of the new herd to arrive, and when news of it had finally come, the nature of the news had scarcely mollified him. To be beholden to Boone Sarsfield for finding and recovering a lost bunch was the last thing Crowley wanted, under present circumstances. Clearly he would almost rather have lost the herd than to have matters develop in such a fashion.

"What business was it of his, that he should go snoopin' and interferin'?" he snarled, then relapsed into a moody silence. Donovan, who had brought the news, had smiled almost contemptuously.

"I don't suppose he did it for love of you," he suggested. "But he's a stubborn cuss, Jeb—mighty near as bull-headed as you when he gets a notion."

"If he thinks that he can come soft-soapin' around me, so that I'll change my mind about killing him, he can think again," Crowley growled. "I could have looked after my own affairs if it hadn't been for him, in the first place."

Donovan made up his mind and turned toward the restaurant. His face, as usual, betrayed none of the thoughts churning busily in his head. It was not that he possessed a poker face; that, he had long since realized, could be a handicap. His face always appeared mobile, reflecting moods or emotions. It served well, like a series of pictures reflected against a window shade, while the curtain effectively concealed what went on within the room.

He was smiling genially as he slid onto a stool, doffing the new white hat as Helen appeared from the kitchen. Familiar now with his habits, she brought a steaming cup of coffee and set it in front of him.

"Good girl," Donovan approved, and eyed her with increasing approval. "I can't wait till you take over out at the ranch," he added. "I'd almost forgotten what real cooking was like." He observed that her glance was taking in his new attire, and felt a shade of disappointment when she calmly refrained from mentioning it.

"As far as going out there to cook is concerned, I'm afraid my answer is still no." Helen shrugged. "Did you want pie?"

"Not today," he denied irritably, though he had been on the point of asking for a piece. His eyes took on a hooded look. This had been part of a game to begin with, one added move in a process as complicated as chess, but the past week had changed all that.

As he'd observed to the owner of the store, it wasn't good for a man to be alone. Ideas long dormant had stirred in his head and heart. He had known a brief hesitation because of the difference in ages, before brushing so trivial a handicap aside. The girl was only about twenty—certainly she couldn't be a day over that, he knew—whereas he was in his middle forties, old enough to be her father. He'd winced when that thought first came to mock him.

Actually, of course, he wasn't old; far from it. He was as strong and active as he'd ever been, not more than half a dozen pounds heavier than he'd been in his twenties, without a gray hair amid the rusty red thatch which for the past several days he'd taken to combing with new care. Why, he was a better man than any of the young sprouts on the range—better than any other, including Jeb Crowley, who lay flat on his back and helpless to protect his own interests.

Even more to the point, he was the owner of Cat-claw, one of the two big outfits. Though some didn't realize it yet, it would be *the* big outfit on a not too distant day. There were occasional disappointments and setbacks—as witness a couple that had taken place in the past week or so. Still, he had a crafty patience which compensated for such reverses.

He gulped the coffee, choked, and pushed the cup away.

"You've been kept pretty busy here ever since you went to work today, haven't you?" he asked abruptly.

"Why, yes, I have been busy," Helen conceded. She was somewhat puzzled at what she sensed was a direct attack.

"I thought so." Donovan nodded. "Quite a lot of things have been happening around town."

"What things? What do you mean?" Something in his manner was disquieting, almost frightening.

Donovan smiled reassuringly. "Well, there ain't been nothing too bad—yet," he added. "I suppose your brother has sent you word, since he got here?"

"Bob?" He saw a flash of what might have been dismay in her eyes. "So that's what some of the men have been talking about—but they break off when they see me. Has something happened?"

"Well, him and the new sheriff came in durin' the night. Hasn't Sarsfield been around, either, after all the nice things you did for him?"

Helen shook her head, hiding her disappoitment. She had heard that Boone was back in town, and she kept watching the door, expecting him to show up. Something must be seriously wrong, and Bob must be involved. Of course, after several days absence, Boone would be busy with a lot of necessary chores—

"You'd better change your mind and take the job working for me," Donovan warned abruptly. "That way, I'd have the right to help you—to look after you." Sudden eagerness was in his voice, a quality of excitement which surprised even himself.

"What I really mean is, I'm askin' you to marry me, Helen. Maybe you've guessed why I've been making the long ride into town every day the way I have. It wasn't to see Crowley—though that's been a good enough excuse. I'm clear crazy about you. You won't have to cook for the crew; only for me—"

He paused at the unconcealed revulsion in her face, the coldness in her eyes. Yielding to impulse, he knew that he had gone too fast. It wasn't like him to forget, to deviate from a well-laid plan, but he was saying only the truth when he admitted that she had gotten into his blood. Even the thought of her engendered an excitement such as had been foreign to his nature for almost two decades.

"I'm offering as much for your sake as my own," he went on. "Give me the right to act for you, and then I'll be able to save your brother from being lynched!"

12.

Helen's eyes had taken on a warning sparkle; her cheeks were an angry red. The color vanished at Donovan's words.

"Lynching—Bob? What do you mean?"

"Just what I say," Donovan assured her with a certain relish. "Likely you don't know what's been happening, and I won't pretend that I do, except that I know what's going on here in town right now. Seems that when the sheriff found that stolen herd of Crowley's, he made an arrest—and the man he brought in was your brother.

"At least that's the way I heard it told. Bob's in jail, and there's lynch talk going around. Folks in this country get right excited about rustlers."

He gave her the news with brutal directness, for that suited his purpose. It was the truth, though he omitted to point out that he had bided his time since coming to town and hearing it. A disgruntled group of people might be turned into a mob, or they might work out their disgruntlement in talk. He had waited to see what would happen here, had made certain that a mob was forming before he broached the subject to Helen. Now there was a real and ugly threat.

Again, her reaction surprised him.

"Why didn't you say so to start with, instead of wasting time?"

Donovan held up a placating hand.

"Whoa now; let's not go off half-cocked," he said. "There's time to handle the situation—only I can do better if I have a right to. I'm not the one that's accusing your brother of being a rustler; I'm only telling you what's been happening, way it's being told. But it does look as though the crowd has pretty well made up its mind."

He had crossed to stare out at the window as he spoke, and, as though impelled against her will, Helen came to stand beside him and watch also. The threat was real enough. The crowd, after gathering in a saloon and liquoring up, had arrived at a point of action. They were streaming out from the saloon, heading toward the sheriff's office and jail, a half-growl, half-shout rising from scores of throats, like the mutter of a multi-headed monster.

"They're moving faster than I counted on," Donovan exclaimed. "I'll have to try and stop them. Give me the right to tell them that he's going to be my brother-in-law, and that could make a big difference—"

Helen seemed not to hear him. This manifestly was not a time for talk, but for action, and she had demonstrated a capacity for that at moments of crisis. She darted to the kitchen, then reappeared, clutching the double barreled shotgun which she had used before.

She was out and running down the street before Donovan realized that she not only had no intention of making him any promise, but that she preferred to depend on herself rather than put any trust in him. Ruefully, he hurried to catch up.

Boone stared wistfully toward The Red Rooster, still closed, then at Ma Jackson's house, equally lacking in any sign of activity. He'd have to wait until people were up, so he might as well take a walk. He was passing an alley when a shadowy figure moved, and something lashed at him, much as had happened when he was descending from the stagecoach. This time, taken off guard, he had no chance to dodge. The blow was smashed hard, and hat and thick hair afforded scant protection. Boone stumbled, then went to his knees. Momentarily he sought to hold fast to the reeling world, to fight back, but the night came sweeping back and over him, as engulfing as a wave. He collapsed without a sound.

He was dreaming, though it was more like a nightmare, requiring a tremendous fight to win back to consciousness. When that was finally achieved, it was as confusing as it was painful. Even worse was the cramped position in which he found himself, because of which for a time he was unable to move.

A musty odor assailed his nostrils, compounded of the smells of a stable, of half-rotten hay, of mice and rats in a long-undisturbed playground. He opened his eyes to half-gloom and was unable to see. Another effort to move, and he had the impression of being caught in a trap.

Breathing was difficult, and then he understood that part of his predicament. He was lying on his back, and a ball of rag had been stuffed in his mouth as a gag. Another strip of cloth ran around his head and was tied in place to keep the gag from being dislodged. His instinctive effort to grab at it was thwarted as his hands refused to move. His arms were behind his back, tied together at the wrists. An effort to thresh with his legs confirmed that they were similarly bound at the ankles.

He tried to shout, but the smothered noise which got past the gag was more like the bawl of a frustrated calf. It seemed unlikely that anyone outside the barn could hear. Even should someone do so, the sound would be hard to place and meaningless.

He was apparently in an old barn, and the gloom,

the inability to see, was due to hay piled around and over him. It must have been in the barn for years. Though not heavy, it was close enough on either side to hold him in place, virtually unable to move.

The ancient, musty quality of the hay suggested that the barn was long unused.

And not a chance in a thousand of anybody finding me—even if someone was looking for me, he reflected. The latter possibility was unlikely, particularly in view of the comings and goings as sheriff, about which he consulted no one.

The worst part was the gag, though the tightly drawn ropes were becoming painful, impeding circulation. With the frantic sense of being trapped, he struggled to free himself, twisting, jerking until he was panting and sweating, all to no avail. Those knots had been tied to hold.

For the first time in his life, Boone was on the verge of panic. It was entirely possible that he could lie there, covered with hay, probably within calling distance of help, until he perished.

Whoever had assaulted him, then bound and gagged him and dragged him back in there, might return in due course to free him. Yet the brutal treatment already accorded him was not reassuring.

The similarity of the two attacks suggested that this one might have been made by the same man who had tried to rob him when he alighted from the stagecoach.

That time, robbery had been the motive. This time, he'd had nothing worth taking.

A possible answer might be that he was the sheriff, and had interfered with the stealing of a herd of cattle. Was some fresh job being planned, and was this a precaution to keep him from bothering?

There were boards underneath him, rather than a dirt floor. Boone tried to shove or hitch along against the pressure of the hay. To his right it was impossible. Here the hay must have lain undisturbed for years. It was lighter on his left, as though it had been forked out of the way before he had been hidden in the pile.

By drawing up his legs and working with elbows and shoulders, after the fashion of an inchworm, he managed to shove forward and sidewise. His head came out from the covering hay into the light. Once the forward shove was under way, he could barely control or check it, and panic gripped him as he lay tense and uncertain.

Part of his body seemed suddenly to be suspended over emptiness. He had the sensation of a precipice.

He was not falling or sliding, and he steadied, taking stock. He was at the edge of the pile of hay, and now he could see overhead and to the sides. Well above him were the rafters of the barn roof; the underside of the cedar shingles was stained and warped. Near one of the beams was a grayish object as big as his head, which he recognized as a yellow-jacket's nest. Apparently it had been long deserted.

At the side, a ladder jutted up, emerging from below, reaching almost to the roof. When the mow at the side, and this space above the stable, were all filled with hay, the ladder would be useful in getting at the tons stored inside the barn. Apparently it had not been put to such use in recent years.

After being tied up, he'd been brought to the second floor, above the part used as a stable. Either his assailant was a powerful man, or he had had help.

Now a part of his body was at the edge of the floor, suspended over the open, empty mow at the side. Should he move farther in that direction, he'd probably plunge to the ground floor.

How far down that might be, it was impossible to judge. It might be only a few feet, but he could not be sure. There were three or four old barns in Singing River, a couple of them squat and ordinary, the others high, according to the predilections of their builders. He had no idea which one he had been brought to.

He considered the possibilities of going on and taking the drop. He might land unhurt on the floor below, but there was always the chance he might crash on the thin edge of a stall, tumbling atop an old plow or cart, and being impaled or badly hurt. Even the prospect of plunging helplessly was terrifying.

On the other hand, if he was unhurt, he might be

able to roll to the street and obtain help. It could prove literally a case of kill or cure.

A pulley was fastened near the roof, and a double rope dangled from it. In that probably lay the explanation of how he had been hoisted to this upper floor.

Studying the situation, Boone lay motionless, reassured that he was in no immediate danger of falling. However, it would be more comfortable back from the brink. He tensed for the effort, then paused. The fingers of one hand had scraped against something sharp and rough.

Feeling it, he decided that it was a nail, bent and only partly driven in. The board was at the edge of the platform, and a rough imperfection, the toughness of a knot, had checked the nail. Hammer blows, glancing off the square head, had roughened and sharpened it. The nail protruded for about an inch.

Such a sharp surface might be the instrument he required to loosen the knots which tied the rope about his wrists. If the knot was snagged on such a hook, it should loosen, after sufficient pulling and tugging.

It would require a lot of hard and painful work; and to get in position, with wrists and knots above the protruding nail, he'd have to lean still farther out, poised above empty space. Ordinarily heights did not worry him, but in his present state of near-helplessness, the prospect was terrifying.

Sucking in as long a breath as the gag permitted, Boone hitched painfully along. It was hardly a matter of choice, for he had to move, before the constricting bonds so impaired his circulation that he'd be log-like and helpless.

The nail rasped against his wrists at least as often as it caught on the knot. For a while it seemed that each time he had it hooked, it pulled loose with no effect. Each jar, however slight, was a breath-stopping event.

The struggle became a nightmare, an endless ordeal in which progress was nil. He was almost ready to give up in despair when a rope slipped, and he kept at it. Finally, after much tugging and wriggling, one wrist came loose.

Working back from the brink, he reached and tore loose the gag, drawing deep breaths in vast relief. Getting his ankles free was still an effort, but now he could use both hands. Finally he was able to stand, then move across to the ladder.

One look at what was below demonstrated the wisdom of the slow and painful course he had pursued. It was considerably farther down than he had expected, and a collection of cast-off articles had gradually accumulated. One was an old plow, a sod-breaker for the prairie, the rusty but still sharp tip of the plowshare where it would have impaled him like a sword.

While he worked, occasional sounds had penetrated, noises of the town, distant but familiar. He shoved the door ajar, then peered out, blinking in surprise at the height of the sun. Apparently he'd lain unconscious for a much longer period than he had realized. By now the day was well along.

The barn was on a back street, where passers-by were rare. The rear of the jail loomed across the way. Farther along, beyond it, he saw the unusual spectacle of a considerable crowd of men debouching from a saloon. A growl of voices blended in angry frenzy, and they swung toward the jail. The purposeful fashion in which they moved was proof enough of their intentions. This was a mob, and they were up to no good.

13.

In spite of the fact that he was bedridden, Jeb Crowley seemed more and more bear-like. He was o uncertain temper, resentful of people and the world i general, and particularly of that part of it which, lik his landlady who also served as a nurse, seemed t want to help him. It was a new and unpleasant experi ence not to be able to do for himself, as galling to hi pride as a saddle-sore.

The news, brought by Pratt Levinger, that his newly purchased herd had been stolen, then recovere through the efforts of Boone Sarsfield, was particu larly unsettling. Here was an unwelcome debt, insul added to injury.

"That's what happens the minute a man ain't abl to tend to things for himself," Crowley choked. "Then that work for you get drunk and loaf!" He glared accusingly at his foreman. "Others steal you blind! And all because I'm in this condition, and with that blasted Sarsfield to thank for being here—"

Mrs. Parrish had been straightening the covers, a gesture which he disrupted by a kick of his good leg. She eyed him over the rims of steel spectacles, a fierce glint in her eyes.

"You also have Mr. Sarsfield to thank for getting your herd back for you, according to what Mr. Levinger has just said," she reminded him tartly.

"And why the devil shouldn't he?" Crowley roared. "Only doing what he's supposed to in his job, ain't he? Got busy at it because he knew the thing was all his fault in the first place. As Mrs. Parrish left the room, he snapped at Levinger, "Get me a pair of crutches!"

"Crutches? What you want with them?" Levinger demurred. "I had to use a pair once, when I was a kid—horse stepped on my foot. They're kind of mean till you get used to them—"

"Who asked your advice? I said to get me a pair."

"Well, sure, sure. Only you're in no shape to try experimentin' with walking, not till your leg's in better shape—"

"Whose leg is it?" Crowley countered. "And who's boss around here, anyhow? Do as I say."

Peabody arose from beside the prone figure of the

sheriff, looking about speculatively. He had worked with swift efficiency, tying and gagging him, and now he stooped and picked the dead weight up with unexpected strength. He might hide him in a clump of grass and brush, or behind a pile of wood. Then his eyes brightened at sight of an old barn, the door standing partly open, grass growing inside. Apparently it had long stood empty.

Discovery of the hay above the stable, the rope and pulley, gave him an added satisfaction. Having hidden the unconscious man to his liking, he was now free to attend to other matters without the risk of interference.

He resisted an impulse to kick the helpless man as he lay there. It would be easy to cave in Sarsfield's ribs, and that would give him strong personal satisfaction. Still, it was unnecessary, for the sheriff would have a sufficiently unpleasant time in the hours to come, and unless he was luckier than he had a right to expect, he might well lie under that old pile of hay for months or even years.

Actually it had not been Sarsfield's fault that the cash robbery had been spoiled, that night when he'd alighted from the stage. Frustration had come about through the interference of the Hankinsons, brother and sister. At the time, there hadn't been much that he could do about it.

That omission, as well as interest on an old score,

would be taken care of within the next few hours. With Boone Sarsfield out of the way, the set-up was perfect for a show which should delight the heart of his employer. And since his boss was paying well, the services rendered might well be extraordinary.

It was always a satisfaction to settle old scores, and this had rankled for a fifth of a century. Not that these young Hankinsons had been directly involved—at least not until they'd chosen to interfere recently. But they were Hankinsons, and that was enough, especially when there was no one else remaining on whom he could wreak vengeance.

Descending the ladder, he let himself out, carefully shutting the door which for so long had stood ajar. Then he sought out a couple of men, carefully chosen and sent on ahead some days before. It would be pleasant to supervise this job himself, but there was other work to be done. Also, it was better to keep out of sight.

There had been a time, a score of years earlier, when he had liked to operate more or less openly, but across the years he had learned caution.

"Free drinks for everybody," he instructed, and was generous with the necessary cash. "One round right after another. You know what to say and how to stir up the crowd. Now get at it."

In the next hour or so, he noted with satisfaction that his lieutenants were doing an excellent job. When

Donovan arrived in town, Peabody was able to report progress and to bring a satisfied sparkle to his employer's eyes.

"The crowd's half-drunk already, and getting worked up to a fighting pitch. They'll soon be ready for anything. Then you can act like a hero, savin' the kid—if you feel so inclined. If you don't—" He shrugged.

"Oh, sure, I'll save him," Donovan agreed. "You really hate him, don't you?" he added curiously.

"Why shouldn't I hate them?" Peabody countered. "The same as yourself," he added pointedly. "Not that either of them ever had anything to do with it—not till lately, anyhow. But the boy's Dad—well, that's past. And it's playing into your hands now, just as you planned. So you can handle things in town. I'll get on out and on with the other jobs. One thing sure, we've been lucky, getting the breaks."

"That's so," Donovan acknowledged. For a moment, in a rare outward show of emotion, his mouth twisted into a snarl. "It's taken a long while, but you know, revenge is twice as sweet when it's long in coming."

"And it'll be a darn sight more profitable, too, as you saw," Peabody added dryly.

Boone reached the jail and slipped inside. Whoever had struck him down in the dawn had taken his gun, but there were weapons in the office, and they had carefully been left untouched. He was not surprised to find the door to the cell padlocked, and Bob Hankinson inside.

Bob arose from the cot, opening his mouth to say something. He changed his mind at sight of Boone, his tone one of quick concern.

"What's wrong, Boone? What's happened to you?"

"Plenty," Boone returned. He was fumbling with the keys, selecting the proper one and fitting it to the lock. "Maybe you'd rather stay inside," he added. "A mob's on the way—and near as I can figure it, you must be their target, though I don't quite know why."

"I could make a guess," Bob said dryly. "Might be wrong, though." He followed Boone back to the office. From outside, the growl of the approaching mob could be heard. "Sounds like they're well worked up."

"They're ugly," Boone agreed. He opened a drawer of the desk and took out a badge, which he pinned on his companion's shirt. Hankinson's eyes widened as he recognized it, but he made no comment. Boone indicated a six-gun in the drawer. He lifted down a shotgun from its pegs as a pounding came at the door.

He was holding the shotgun as he threw open the door, Bob at his side. The still oncoming mob, at least half a hundred men, stuttered to a sudden halt at sight of the leveled guns. Most of them, Boone noted grimly, clutched a half-emptied liquor bottle in one hand.

Helen Hankinson, coming behind them and unnoticed, caught her breath. Then she took her old stand on the steps of the post office, clutching her own scatter-gun, waiting unobtrusively.

It required only a look to be certain that someone had worked efficiently on the passions of the group. They had been worked up to a murderous pitch, but to be met in such fashion had not been in their calculations. Peabody's lieutenants, now carefully in the background, had been assured that they would meet with no interference, least of all from the sheriff.

"Well?" Boone challenged. The shotgun was carelessly leveled to cover most of the group.

Men shuffled uneasily. One, pushed forward by others who were reluctant to be in the limelight, proved an unwilling spokesman.

"Reckon you know what we want, Sarsfield—an' who we want."

"How should I know that?" Boone countered. "Somebody slugged me from behind early this morning, then left me tied up in an old barn. I've just gotten loose."

The haggard lines of his face, covered with sweat and grime, the raw and lacerated wrists, clearly visible as he held the shotgun, gave mute proof that he had indeed endured an ordeal. Their original enthusiasm was fast draining from the surprised and discomfited mob.

"What did you have in mind?" Boone prodded.

"Well—nothin' much, I guess. But that man 'side of you there—the one you arrested as a rustler—"

"A rustler?" Boone repeated. "Hankinson here? Somebody must be crazy. I didn't arrest him. He helped me get back the stolen herd. Who's been stringin' you with such a line?"

"But you had him locked in a cell back there. Some of us looked in this morning and saw him—"

"We got into town late last night, and I slept on the cot in the office and he slept on a cot in one of the cells. The cell wasn't locked. Somebody—likely whoever it was that slugged me—must have locked it while Bob was still asleep."

Waiting only a moment for that to penetrate their liquor-fogged minds, he added sharply:

"You'll notice he's wearing a badge as deputy sheriff. That tells what I think of him. Somebody's been bound and determined to stir up trouble, and I'll be interested in finding out who it was! Now, you fellows disperse. There'll be no mob law in this town while I'm sheriff!"

14.

As the breath eased from her pent-up lungs in a long sigh, Helen stepped down from the post office porch and hurried back to The Red Rooster, tingling with pride though still baffled by lack of understanding. But at any rate, she knew enough, and this time there had been no need for her to interfere. It was better so.

From another vantage-point, Donovan had watched with equal amazement and much less pleasure. Still, he decided, it might be as well that Peabody's plan had not quite succeeded. The most disturbing factor was the unexpected appearance of Boone Sarsfield, and the way he had handled the situation. The man was becoming a nuisance, and worse; he was going to require some thought.

Outwardly pleased, Donovan returned to make a report to Crowley on what had occurred. Since others would bear the same tale, he gave it with reasonable accuracy and few embellishments.

"Oh, and I've got a piece of news for you," he added, as if it were an afterthought, "something I figure you'll be interested in. Who do you think I caught a glimpse of this morning? Sure surprised me, but Peabody's back in town."

"Peabody?" Crowley repeated incredulously. He grew still, his face whitening. "You mean—?"

"Him," Donovan agreed. "He's changed some, has a full set of whiskers now and is a bit older, of course, but he hadn't changed enough to fool me. I just thought you might like to know."

Crowley continued silent, pondering, obviously shaken, and Donovan allowed him time. It was now more than twenty years since Elisha Peabody had first turned up in Singing River, a traveling man with a certain dash and fascination.

At least, he must have had such qualities to cause Crowley's wife of only a few months to run off with him. That she had also, not long afterward, run away from him somewhere in the East, was no longer relevant, as long as Jeb Crowley was concerned.

That incident had marked a turning point in the lives of many people, but only a few old-timers in the Singing River country remembered. Crowley, from an amiable giant, had been transformed into a vengeful, embittered man.

"Peabody? You're sure? What would he be doing back in this country?" His real thoughts came to the fore as he glared at his outstretched leg on the bed. "Blast this foot!" he swore. "Just when a man needs to be able to be up and about, to stomp a whole nest of rattlers—"

"Now, now, Jeb, maybe I oughtn't to have told you. Just take it easy—"

"Take it easy? Are you crazy? But I've told Pratt to get me a pair of crutches. And with them and a gun—"

"Whoa now, man!" Donovan protested. "Seems like you're bound to commit suicide. Can't you get it through that thick head of yours, Jeb, that for one thing Sarsfield ain't just sheriff; he's a tough coyote as well? And he might be teamin' up with Peabody, for all we know—"

"Likely he is, but who cares?" Crowley stormed. "I promised that I'd kill him, and I'll do it—both of them, if I have to. When I say something, I mean it."

"Could be that Sarsfield'll be sharpenin' up on his own marksmanship." Donovan shrugged, but he was not displeased. Crowley would almost certainly remove the man who was fast becoming a threat. The sheriff would be hesitant in returning the gunfire of a man on crutches. Should he be forced to do so, that would also be a desirable result.

The cumulative interest on old accounts seemed

finally in a fair way to be paid. If there were certain dividends, not originally contemplated, that was all to the good.

Boone led the way to the restaurant. Bob was silent as usual, a young man with a ready smile but few words. Helen was waiting as they entered, and her eyes went from one to the other, blinking momentarily as though tears were not far from the surface. But her greeting was prosaic enough.

"I suppose you're hungry," she said.

"We're starved," Boone agreed. "I saw you at the post office again," he added, as he slid onto a stool.

Helen colored. "I hope no one else noticed."

Having anticipated their coming, she had food ready to set before them, and they gave their full attention to the viands. Boone eyed his companion curiously as they walked back to the office.

"I sort of thought you and your sister might like to visit together," he suggested.

"She's my half-sister," Bob explained. "Maybe she'd rather have talked to *you*," he added.

That remark eliciting no reply, he tried another tack.

"You sure you want me to wear this badge?" he asked. "I sure appreciate it—everything you've done. But now that the excitement's over—"

Boone had been giving serious thought to the matter. It had been a sudden impulse, pinning a badge on Hankinson, partly to show the mob what he thought of their way of acting. He had rightly gauged that it would be the last thing they would expect.

The ruse had worked, but there remained some unanswered questions, and Bob seemed as reticent as ever about furnishing them. Nonetheless, Boone was satisfied with the course he'd taken. Brother and sister alike had stood by him when he'd needed friends; a man could do not less in return.

"Since I've got it," Bob added, glancing diffidently at his star, "I'd like to ride out again, if you don't mind—do some more looking around, try and keep an eye on what's happening, or might happen—before it gets too big."

"Might be a good idea," Boone agreed soberly. "You any idea what might happen, as you put it?"

"Wish I did," Bob confessed. "Knowing what to look for would help a lot. As it is, about all that we can do is be on the watch."

"You had a reason for coming to this country in the first place?" Boone probed.

"Sure did." His smile, as always, was warm; his glance, as usual, remained diffident. "I came out figuring I'd have to kill somebody. But if I do, I promise you one thing. I won't use the badge as a shield to hide behind."

The next day, Levinger brought the crutches which Crowley had ordered.

"They look as though they'd be strong enough, anyway," he explained uneasily. "I couldn't find a pair in town, so had to get some made. They aren't exactly what I had in mind."

Crowley snorted, taking a crutch in either hand. "You had them made for a horse?" he demanded, but he was not displeased. They were of iron, pipes with a curved arm piece welded at the top, and those crossbars had been padded with layers of sheep pelt, to which the wool still adhered. Clearly, they were the handiwork of the blacksmith.

"About what I'd expect, even to the wool," Crowley added, but found them solid and not too heavy for his mighty arms. He swung himself to the edge of the bed, balancing; then, sweating, and with Levinger's aid, he heaved himself erect, onto his one good leg. Not until he had twice traveled the length of the room did he fall back into bed, exhausted but triumphant.

"Another two or three days of exercisin' with these things, and I'll be good enough to walk out of here," he said. "Then we'll see about a few matters."

His landlady appeared in the doorway, vigilant of eye and, as usual, uncompromising of tongue.

"You're sure anxious to commit suicide, ain't you?" she asked. "Fair pantin' for it, like a dog chasin' its tail. And as for you, Pratt Levinger, I'd think you'd be proud of yourself, aidin' and abettin' a sick man in such foolishness!"

Levinger looked unhappy, but there was nothing that he could say. Crowley made up for his taciturnity.

"As long as he takes my pay, he does what I tell him," he snapped. "And I'll remind *you*, ma'am, that I'm paying for my keep here!"

"The same as for a fat hog or steer, you mean? At least I'd keep them properly penned while on the premises!"

Crowley exploded with sudden laughter. The sound was so unexpected that both his hearers were startled.

"Ma'am, you've got something there," he conceded. "You know, you're the first woman—or man—that ever gave me back as good as I sent. And don't think that I'm not appreciative of the things you've done for me here, Mis' Parrish. I am. I know I've been a complainin' aggravation, and I wouldn't blame you for throwing me out. But what's a man to do in a situation like this? My way's always been to stick to my friends and to tromp my enemies!"

"He's pathetic," Mrs. Parrish confided to Levinger, as the foreman was taking his leave. "The poor misguided man! And the worst part is that he can't tell the difference between his real friends and his worst enemies!"

15.

It was common knowledge in the town that Jeb Crowley was getting about on his crutches, spending more and more time practicing each day. He intended to become at home on them, strong enough to venture out of doors. And when that day came, he'd sally forth with a gun in his hand. To fulfill the promise he'd made to kill the sheriff which had become an obsession with him.

"You sure he's the man you want to kill?" Mrs. Parrish startled him by demanding. Balancing on crutches, breathing heavily, Crowley glared at her in amazement.

"Who elses have I promised to kill lately?" he demanded. "You implyin' that I'm getting absent-minded about such things?"

"He's plumb cantankerous," Donovan admitted to Helen, on one of his regular pilgrimages to town and the restaurant. "When he's in such a mood, there's just no arguing with him. And it's too bad. He's good-hearted, Jeb is—good-hearted as they come."

"And he shows it by trying to murder someone?" Helen retorted fiercely.

"Don't get him wrong," Donovan protested. "He doesn't look at it that way. They'll both have their guns, makin' it a fair fight, as he sees it. Oh, I know how it looks to most people, how it really is. He ought to be man enough to admit he made a mistake, shake hands, and even say thank you for favors rendered. Likely you could do it that way, maybe even I could, but not Jeb. Somehow he's never been able to bring himself to do such a thing, not in all his born days. Be good for him if he would—" He shook his head soberly. "He's always been my best friend"

And you've always been his worst enemy! Helen thought, but did not say the words aloud. Jeb Crowley at least was forthright, honest according to the yardstick he had set up for himself. She was sick with apprehension at what seemed certain to happen, but at least such forthrightness was preferable to the circuitous methods pursued by the unctuous boss of the Catclaw.

The very name of the outfit seemed symbolic. One could claw and scratch, covering sharp and rasping noises with a falsely overloud purr. There was peril in the air, blood on the moon, and the worst part was that she did not know what to do, nor could she hit upon any feasible plan for stopping the inevitable.

A dozen times she had been on the point of appealing to Boone to do something, but she had choked back the words, realizing that even a mild plea might cost him his life.

Forthright in her ways, even headstrong—a trait somewhat reminiscent of Crowley—Helen had arrived at certain conclusions, none of which was pleasant or satisfying. Nor was there anyone to whom she could turn in the crisis. Even Bob was away. She had often found his methodical approach to problems an aggravation, but she had to admit that in the end his judgment was usually sound.

For the first time in her life she felt frustrated, at a loss as to what to do. Color rushed hotly to her cheeks as she pondered, admitting the reason for her concern. Already she had been almost brazen in backing Boone Sarsfield so publicly, when other women would have shrunk from such a course. But he had been in danger—

He was in even greater danger now, and she would do as much again, if only she could determine what might be helpful, rather than a hindrance. With such men involved, it would be easy to make a bad situation worse. Boone would be reluctant to protect himself by killing his former employer, a man whom he still regarded as a friend. On crutches, Crowley would appear a partial cripple, deserving of sympathy, even special consideration—

Such a sense of chivalry might lead Boone to his own destruction. Under any circumstances, that would be bad enough, but in these particular ones it would be unbearable.

Again she wondered if she should go to Crowley, ask him to change his mind, to drop what he had promised to do. As a woman, young, and conscious of her own beauty, she could make a powerful appeal. Yet such a plea might easily do more harm than good.

The door of The Red Rooster jerked open, and a half-grown boy stuck his head inside. His voice shrilled with excitement.

"You better get outside if you want to see the fun. Jeb Crowley's coming out! He's sent word to Sarsfield that he's on his way to kill him!"

The boy was gone again on his self-appointed mission as the messenger of evil tidings, the door slamming behind him. Helen stood a moment, a hand above her heart, her face suddenly drained of blood. Her gaze ranged frantically to the double barreled shotgun resting on elk antlers above the stove in the kitchen. She had twice borrowed the old twelve-gauge without the consent but with the tacit approval of her employer. Would it serve a third time? Slowly she shook her head. Today it was not the answer—no matter what happened.

The street at first sight appeared to be deserted, as though the hour were dawn rather than mid-afternoon.

A single saddled horse slumbered at a hitch-rail, head drooping to match its tail. Some of the homesteaders had been in town less than an hour before, loading supplies at The Hardluck Mercantile, getting more lumber at the mill at the edge of the town. Now they were on their way back to their land, the brief flurry of activity over and the dust all settled.

Such townspeople or visitors as might ordinarily move along the street had suddenly found reasons for taking shelter inside buildings, out of the line of possibly flying lead. From open windows and doors slightly ajar, most of the population were watching, but they did so in a hushed expectancy, like the slowing of a heartbeat.

Only two people were openly visible, the two most vitally interested in this drama of life or death.

Jeb Crowley had come into the open air, for the first time since he'd been carried, unwillingly, inside Mrs. Parrish's house. He moved slowly on the crutches, more than ever resembling a grizzly bear in his shambling gait. For the first time since his fall, he had donned gun and belt. The revolver caught the reflection of the sun, sending back flashes like signals.

After being shut away from the sun for ten days, Crowley's habitual tan had faded to a strange pallor, but the color clearly was no indication of lack of purpose. He paused a moment, blinking against the brightness, hearing the snarl of quarreling dogs, a sound in tune with his own mood.

Boone Sarsfield came from the sheriff's office to the street, pausing momentarily, then shrugging resignedly. Since Crowley had sent word that he was coming, he could not very well refuse to meet him. This affair, declared and well publicized, had become bigger than both of them.

Boone was reluctant in his own mind as to the proper course to pursue. He had not really expected that his efforts in getting back the stolen herd would make any difference to Jeb Crowley. He had merely been heaping coals of fire on Jeb's head, and those had a habit of proving highly uncomfortable, of inflaming passions to an ever greater degree. Not that he'd done it with any such notion in mind.

Jeb Crowley, as the result of a succession of events, had had to act and react, one way or another. Even disregarding his public challenge and declaration of intent, it had become a matter of principle with him never to change his mind.

Today he was devil-driven, hating the task he had set himself, yet stubbornly determined to carry through. That he might die in the process worried him not at all. He'd shoot to kill, exactly as he had threatened. And Jeb Crowley's gun rarely missed.

Boone had considered riding out from town again for several days, but that would be no solution; only a postponement. To shoot to kill in turn might or might not save his own life. Anything less would probably lose it.

The sun was warm, and he found himself sweating as he saw Crowley start his painful hobbling toward a meeting place somewhere in the middle of the street. Eb Callendar had used new pipes for the crutches, and they shone in the sun, rivaling the gleam of the gun. The barking of dogs came again, the only sound to break the sudden stillness. The birds, whose swirling wings had filled field and town only a week before, had vanished in a night.

Boone suspected that they'd halt and palaver briefly before going for their guns. Both were bound by the code which insisted that each should be ready before the other started his draw. The custom was a concession to fair play, though in practice it seldom worked that way. Almost always, in a gun fight, one man was faster, or surer, or more coldbloodedly determined than his opponent. Whatever the appearance, such encounters were rarely more than a prelude to murder.

Talk would delay but not alter the situation. Boone knew Jeb Crowley too well for that.

Boone swallowed, his throat dry. However short, this promised to be the longest walk he'd ever taken. He could see The Red Rooster farther down the street. Helen would be there, her own heart in her throat; that soft, round, white throat in which he'd seen a pulse beat, or color rise richly to tint cheeks and forehead a hue matching her ripe lips. . . .

Today there was nothing that Helen could do, nothing that anyone could do. That was one of the mockeries of talk; that people could mouth words which were clear in each other's ears, yet still not be able to communicate, to make sense or reason, although each might wish desperately to do so. It was so much easier to resort to force, to a situation explosive with hatred.

Helen. He'd known her less than two weeks, yet those two weeks had compassed all that seemed important in life. Now life might be drawing to a sudden end.

A dozen times he'd been tempted to tell her how he felt, to ask her to marry him; he had even toyed with the wild notion of suggesting that they might ride away in the night, leaving all this behind. It had been an effort, realizing what he might gain or lose, to hold fast to his manhood.

She would probably despise him if he voiced such thoughts; certainly he would hate himself. So, knowing that this hour lay ahead, all the words of hope or promise had gone unspoken.

Now the hour was at hand. Crowley had halved the distance. As a matter both of custom and courtesy, Boone had to go at least part way to meet him. That was a strange sort of politeness, for men whose motive was to kill.

Crowley was sweating also. Boone could see it on his face, perspiration drawn to the surface not entirely by the warmth of the sun. The big man halted, planting both crutches firmly, balancing himself carefully. He released his grip with his right hand, swearing softly. The iron was growing unpleasantly warm. He rubbed the palm across the front of his shirt to wipe away the sweat. That way, his fingers poised only inches above the holstered revolver.

"Thought you aimed to make me walk all the way," he snarled. "Figured to tire me to the point where I couldn't shoot straight, eh?"

"This was your idea, Jeb," Boone returned. "I've no quarrel with you—no reason for killing you."

"Well, I've reason for killing *you*," Crowley retorted. "Nobody interferes with me as you've done and gets away with it. And there ain't no point to wastin' words!"

Whatever else he was, Crowley was game, with courage enough to carry through, no matter how many butterflies might dash about wildly inside him. If his own sensations were any indication, Boone suspected that Crowley must be equally human. His trouble was a stubbornness which knew no other way.

He'd said the final word, and he was going for his gun. Boone still hesitated, reluctant to follow suit, knowing that to tarry would mean to go down again into such awful darkness as had twice overtaken him, a night this time without dawn.

Then it happened, the impossible for which he'd hoped despairingly. The barking and snarling dogs erupted in a sudden violent clamor, and half a dozen mixed breeds, fighting among themselves, spewed from the alley, surging around and against Crowley. One shot blasted from his gun, but it sailed high as he spilled, the unsteady crutches knocked from under him by the surging rush. The dogs swept over him and on, out of sight. Crowley remained sprawled.

Boone was the first to reach him, though Helen was but an instant behind. For once, Jeb Crowley was strangely silent, his face washed white with pain and shock.

It was not much wonder that even so tough an old ranny had fainted. The angle of his once injured limb indicated clearly that the partly knitted bone had snapped again.

16.

Not even his enemies, had they planned it—and by
now, Crowley included most men in that vague but
sweeping generalization—could have subjected him to
a worse humiliation or greater anticlimax. To be felled
ingloriously by a pack of quarreling hounds was to
him the ultimate in insults.

"I've been put upon, one way and another, till it's
become unbearable," he exploded to Donovan, and
shook both fists at the ceiling. His neighbor had been
prompt to make the journey to town upon word of the
accident, was full of sympathy for the mishap.
"There's a limit to what a man should be called on
to take, and I'm long past it."

He moved his great shoulders restlessly, closing
and unclosing hands in hungry fashion. His glare
focused on the bulge made by the newly set and
splintered leg. The comments of the resummoned
medico had been pointedly caustic.

"Old fool says that I'll have to stay here in bed now

for at least a month, 'fore I even try to get out, or it could be I'll never walk again," Jeb gritted. "But if he thinks I'll accept everything lyin' down—well, without fighting back, if anybody thinks that, they can sure as shooting figure again!"

"That could be too much to expect," Donovan soothed. "After all, when it comes to a fight, you've got a good crew behind you. Or if they ain't good enough—"

The bait was both tempting and timely. Crowley considered the idea a moment, chewing it over like a dog with a new bone. He beckoned Donovan closer, lowering his voice.

"You know, Rusty, sometimes you come up with an idea. Sure I'll fight. But maybe that tame crew I've got *ain't* good enough. Still, like you say, I can get some that are—men who know how to use guns and ain't afraid to pull the trigger! What I want you to do—"

Donovan heard his request without surprise, having carefully planted the various threads of the idea on half a dozen different visits. Now he appeared to hesitate.

"Whatever you say, Jeb—if that's what you're sure you want. In some ways, it sounds sort of drastic. But you know I'll back you."

"Yeah, I reckon I do," Crowley conceded. Momentarily, the craggy lines of his face softened. "You've always stood by me, no matter what—exceptin' the time we both made fools of ourselves for the same reason, and that time you came to your senses quicker'n I did. Now I have to depend on you. Levinger would be no good for what I want. But I'm in a hurry. You sure you can manage?"

"I'll find a way to work it. Can't let you down at a time like this. Fact is, maybe you're luckier'n you think. There's some fellows out of a job, just drifted this way—I'll see can I round them up. Only this will cause considerable of a ruction, you know that."

"A ruction's what I want, and then some. I'm not going to stand for no more trespassin' on my rights, either on Moon Star or here in town. This'll be just a first step. All right; it's up to you. Crippled up the way I am, I've got to depend on somebody, and who else can I trust?"

"Now that's a good question," Donovan admitted, observing that, as usual, Crowley failed to detect the irony in his statement.

FOR the past several days, work had been progressing on new houses on the six homesteads, shelters being built against the threat of the coming winter. As had been the case from the time of the first arrivals, everything seemed to go faster on the Martin place. There the scars of fire and destruction had been all but covered.

Laurie Martin shifted her weight on the roof,

stretching cramped but shapely limbs, fetchingly revealed in a pair of her husband's Levis. She had been hesitant about donning such garments, then, with a determined nod of the head, had struggled into them. She could nail shingles as well as any man, and a tight roof over their heads was an urgent need. Moreover, hoop skirts were not only inappropriate for such exercise, but were impossible for climbing ladders. In any case, there would be no one around to see.

The hour was just short of sunset, the air clear and warm, with a washed, fresh look, as though it had been morning instead of evening. Laurie paused, hammer suspended above a nail, gazing into the distance. Well to the north, the hills shone blue in the haze of dusk, and willows, following the meandering line of Singing River, were dancing in red, with the sudden loss of the summer's leafy cover.

Thereabouts, as she knew, was the border between Moon Star and Catclaw. And though the distance was several miles, the range of vision was excellent.

Paul Martin, climbing the ladder with a bundle of shingles balanced on one shoulder, dropped them on the roof with a thud and a sigh of relief.

"Seems like those bundles weigh twice as much as they did in the morning," he observed. "But this is the last one. Ought to finish the roof. What you looking at, honey?"

Cattle," Laurie explained, and gestured with the hammer.

"Cattle?" Paul followed her gaze, nodding. "Looks like quite a herd—riders moving them along, too. That's kind of queer, this time of day."

"That's what I thought." Laurie continued to watch, her voice troubled. "It's a *huge* herd," she added. "Why, almost all the Moon Star bunch must be right there."

Martin frowned at the mass, which looked like a spreading drop of ink, was being absorbed by a blotter. In this case, they were disappearing in the wide-fringing swamp of willows.

"Who cares about Moon Star one way or the other?" he asked irritably.

"We do—when somebody interferes with Moon Star cattle, and we get blamed for what happens," Laurie reminded him.

Her husband regarded her soberly, shifting his attention from the vanishing herd to her face and back again. He had heard about the butchered calf, for which they had been unjustly accused.

"I don't understand what you're bothered about," he protested. "Those are Moon Star cattle, right enough, but they're on Moon Star range, and driven by Moon Star cowboys. What's wrong about that?"

"Three things might be wrong," Laurie pointed out. "In the first place, those men can't be the crew from Moon Star. I noticed almost the entire crew riding past on their way to town this afternoon—and they haven't returned. Anyway, why should Moon Star cattle be driven off their own range onto Catclaw—and just as night is coming down?"

Martin pondered those statements a full minute. Then he commenced to back down the ladder.

"Reckon I'll stick my neck out," he decided. "I'll take a horse and try and get word to someone on Moon Star. We could be wrong—maybe there's nothing to it. But it will do no harm to be sure."

"At least they'll understand that we're trying to be friendly, and that we appreciate this lumber and being given another chance," Laurie agreed, and drove in a nail with a quick hard stroke of the hammer.

She descended from the roof when darkness made it impossible to continue work, and the nose-tickling fragrances of supper were filling the not quite completed cabin by the time that Paul Martin returned. He noted with approval that she had again donned dress and apron. Undeniably, she was good-looking in Levis, but he found the whole notion vaguely unsettling.

"Did you get word to them?" Laurie asked.

"More or less. I couldn't find any of the Moon Star crew—guess they're still in town. But I met Sarsfield's new deputy and told him what we'd seen. He as right interested."

The newcomer rapped timidly at the outer door, then, upon being admitted, slipped almost diffidently into the room where Crowley lay, twiddling a huge hat uncertainly in both hands. To the critical gaze of Mrs. Parrish, he seemed to be one of those destined to inherit the earth, if meekness was a requisite. He bowed politely, and his tone, unlike that of the angry boss of Moon Star, was soft and restrained. At least, Mrs. Parrish decided, the man wasn't a trouble-maker.

Had she guessed that the stranger was there in response to Crowley's summons, delivered through Donovan, she might have viewed him with a more jaundiced eye. She was becoming increasingly distrustful both of Rusty and his visits, her liking for the man waning as his own spirits seemed to improve.

Standing in the door of his office, Boone Sarsfield also took note of the man as he came to town, then rode out again, having made the single call. Always a noticing man, it had been painfully borne in upon the sheriff that vigilance was the price of existence.

Aside from the fact that the newcomer chose to visit Crowley, Boone found nothing suspicious in the incident; not, at least, until that period between sunset and the coming of full night, when a dozen men came riding casually into town. They had the look of cowboys, insofar as dress was concerned, but all were strangers to Singing River—save the man at their head, who had made the earlier call upon Crowley.

They differed in other respects from ordinary cowboys, a certain hardness in face and manner matching the twin guns which most of them carried. Several had rifles in saddle sheaths in addition.

Watching their arrival, Boone sighed, pushing up from his chair. Even without the clue of the call that had been made upon Crowley, he could tell that this was manifestly an open challenge to his authority.

Following the dispersal of the mob a few days earlier, Boone had issued an edict governing conduct within the town. It was not new, having first been promulgated perhaps a score of years earlier, but in that time it had become rusty from disuse. It was to the effect that guns were not to be worn or carried in the town. All who came with weapons had to leave them at the sheriff's office for the duration of their stay. When they were ready to ride out, the guns could be reclaimed.

The order was neither unusual nor unreasonable. Most towns had a similar rule, for the protection of their citizens and the keeping of the peace. The fact that the old edict had gone more or less disregarded in Singing River did not alter the circumstances.

None of this new crew was making any move to turn in at the office or to comply with the regulation.

learly, they were flaunting their guns, defying the
w, at Crowley's order.

Jeb's sure cantankerous—not to say silly, Boone re-
ected, but he felt as much sympathy for his former
oss as irritation. Jeb had succeeded in backing him-
lf into a corner, and that was the worst possible
tuation, especially for a man of overweening pride.
here was no one else to push around so he could
et out, which did not prevent him from trying.

Boone found the newcomers in the big saloon
sually favered by Moon Star when its crew came to
wn. None of the regular riders from the ranch was
ere tonight. All of them had been in the evening
efore, orderly and well-behaved. This seemed more
ke a masquerade, of sheep in the garb of wolves.
r were they as wolfish as they seemed at pains to
emonstrate?

Boone paused inside the door. As though to make
ure that there should be no misunderstanding, the
ild-mannered man of earlier in the day shouldered
p to the bar, rapping loudly with the stock of his
evolver, demanding service. His voice rose, harshly
rrogant.

Not satisfied with the prompt response, he twirled
e gun by the trigger guard, flipping it into the air,
atching it expertly and shooting, all in one rolling
otion. The neck of a whiskey flask, perched on the
ighest shelf behind the bar, was neatly cut off with·

out any of the contents spilling.

Boone sauntered forward.

Heads swung. The newcomers waited expectantly
even leeringly. The half-dozen regular patrons o
the bar, who had hesitated to make a sudden exodus
sought to crowd toward the rear.

"Good shooting," Boone observed blandly. "Now
that that's been demonstrated, I'll take your guns."

"The devil you will!" It was the meek man wh
answered, strangely transformed. All at once he wa
as wild and rangy in appearance as a Texas steer
and just as obviously from that uncurried state. "No
body takes my gun, mistuh!"

"Or mine," a redheaded compaion backed him, and
toyed with the Colt's in his own hand. "Strikes me w
might take your'n, though, Sheriff!"

Boone surveyed them. There had been no real ques
tion in his mind, but now all doubts were resolved
They had been hired to make trouble. Crowley woulc
cheerfully pay each of them a month's wage for this
one evening if they made their defiance stick.

"I said I'd take your guns," he repeated. "You ca
have them again when you're ready to ride out." He
moved forward, confronting the leader and extend
ing a hand.

It could have gone either way. He saw a flicker o
doubt in pale eyes, and in that instant Eb Callenda
spoke from the doorway. The blacksmith was looking

at the roomful of men across the leveled double barrels of a shotgun.

"I hope you boys won't do nothing to disturb my trigger finger," he explained almost apologetically. "But the rest of us hereabouts, we figured it was about time for us to start backin' our sheriff, after helpin' put him in that job!"

17.

It had been more the glint in his eye than his actual words, as Bob Hankinson thanked Martin, which told the homesteader that the deputy sheriff was more than casually interested in the news he brought. Rarely did Hankinson betray his feelings in words.

He lost no time in riding north to Catclaw, to that remote section where the herd had last been seen. And there, somewhat surprisingly, they were. Looking at the huge herd, most of them asleep under a waning moon, Bob was puzzled as to exactly what was going on. That something was happening, virtually under his nose and in full view of any who might care to watch, he was certain. But none of the usual procedures in thievery were being followed.

This was virtually the entire herd of Moon Star, from young calves to old cows, with the main beef herd of steers in between. Scattered among them were the yearlings which Sarsfield had purchased, then recovered after their abortive dash for the border. They had become assimilated with the main herd, feeling at home among them.

The entire bunch had been rounded up and moved north, off regular Moon Star range, and not by any of the regular crew who drew Crowley's pay. Now they loitered on a broad but hidden meadow, partly encompassed by a wide loop of the river, partly encircled by mountains cloaked darkly by evergreens.

No one was riding night herd, nor did anyone appear to be on guard. The nature of the terrain would discourage any tendency to stray, at least for a few days. The river offered plenty of water, and the pasture was knee deep.

The significant factor, in Hankinson's mind, was that from here striking straight on north, traveling across Catclaw, then on open range, it was only a quick dash to the border. The yearlings, once stolen, had gotten that far, only to be recovered through Boone Sarsfield's intervention. Here was a far bigger, more valuable bunch, unguarded, ready for the taking.

Yet, having come this far, they had been left unwatched. Why?

There had to be an answer, and much might hinge upon it. Hankinson set out to find it.

Crowley, confined to his bed, denied even the solace of hobbling about on crutches, had made a startling discovery. Surprisingly, he realized that he had a mind with which to think.

Now, with little else that he could do to occupy himself, he fell to meditating, remembering the events of the past, pondering the possible foolishness of the course which he had followed with so little deviation across the years. Never before had he been plagued by self-doubt; but then, never before had he really stopped to think.

Always he had acted on impulse, justifying the course he took in his own mind, never delving too deeply. It could be, he decided, that there was a great and, for him, hitherto unsuspected difference between emotionalism and real thought; it might even be that he had been a first-class chump, possibly many times.

The tale, brought him by his landlady, of how a wild gun crew had ridden into town the evening before, challenging the sheriff's rule against carrying weapons, and how Boone Sarsfield had handled them, left Crowley strangely shamed. Perhaps no one but himself knew of his part in that episode—or at least Donovan would not mention it. Still, it had been a foolish gesture, even reprehensible.

He was in a deflated mood, almost humble, when Pratt Levinger came storming in.

For the past couple of weeks, Levinger had behaved strangely. The near loss of the yearlings, the night spent locked in a cell, had given him both common sense and time to think, and some of his reflections had not fed his vanity. The resultant reticence in words and action had aroused his employer's ire, until he had finally hired another crew, who would be more ready to do his bidding. That was probably the explanation. And it was that second crew and its behavior which now had angered the foreman.

"What the devil do you think you're about?" he demanded, in a tone which no one, at least no man, by Crowley's own confession, had ever used with him before. "I heard about that gun crew here in town last night, and how they tried to start trouble. And I know about McQuillan—who was leading them, *after* calling on you during the afternoon!"

Crowley sought, not to successfully, to clutch fast the remnants of dignity and authority.

"What if he did call on me?" he growled.

"Just this. You hired that crew to get Boone. Without going into the right or wrong of belittlin' the law, let me ask you this. Am I foreman, or ain't I? If you want to try running the outfit from your bed here, say so, and the devil with it. I'll ride out. But while I'm foreman, I do the hiring and firing, and I have to know what's going on. I won't have another crew working behind my back!"

To his surprise, and almost his consternation, Crowley surrendered weakly.

"All right," he conceded. "I guess maybe you've got a gripe. I just wasn't thinking straight, hiring them that way. Fact is," he went on, "may-be I haven't been doing much straight thinking for a long spell—too long."

Levginer eyed him anxiously.

"Are you all right?" he asked. "You must have a fever, or something. Maybe I better send for the doctor again, to take another look at you."

Crowley grimaced. "I ain't feverish," he denied. "Not this time. The trouble with me, I reckon, is that I've been seven different varieties of a fool, one time and another. Only I never stopped to think, before. I held to my mad, and made out like that was reason enough. It was a fool trick to chase off the nesters, and a sight worse to burn them out. Boone was right when he said he didn't want none of that."

Levinger sank onto a chair beside the bed. His own burst of wrath and words had evaporated before this unexpected contrition on the part of his employer.

"Trying to shoot him, after he'd done his duty as sheriff—and done a good job—that was even crazier," Crowley went on inexorably. "Then getting those fellows in to make trouble—without telling you—well, I wouldn't blame you for quitting me flat, Pratt. Only I'd sure be up against it if you did."

"You know," Levinger observed soberly, "I think

you must be getting better."

"About time, ain't it? Anyhow, I've quit meddlin'. You're runnin' things. Do whatever you think best."

"I will," Levinger agreed. "I was all set to quit, I was so mad, except for one thing. Yesterday afternoon, a couple of the boys rode out to check on the herd, some as usual. They didn't get back till after dark—and I couldn't believe that they reported. They couldn't find any of the cattle."

"Couldn't find them?" Crowley leaned on an elbow. "How do you mean, they couldn't? Why, they couldn't stray—and they sure wouldn't wander far—"

"All I know is that they were all there, where they were supposed to be, on the last check a couple of days before. Now they're gone. I've got everybody out riding. I'll fire that other bunch that were packin' guns here in town. I have a notion that maybe they're mixed up in this, somehow."

"They couldn't have had anything to do with it," Crowley protested. "How could they?" He moved pettishly. "Just when I need to ride, here I'm flat on my back—"

He grimaced, then, surprisingly, grinned.

"I'm not blaming you, Pratt. I know you're doing a good job, and you'll find them. And if you need help—well, I guess there's the sheriff."

"I was thinking of him," Levinger confessed. "One thing sure, something almighty queer's going on!"

Queer, as a term, might well be an understatement, Levinger reflected. Many recent events had left him bewildered. It was more instinct than the evidence of his senses which assured him that a cat and mouse game was being played, with Moon Star in the middle. The cook, also troubled, had expressed Levinger's feelings accurately, if somewhat ambiguously, by declaring that things were getting no better fast.

Nearing the border of Moon Star, after the long and tiring ride back from town, Levinger was met with the word that the missing herd had been found. Two of the crew, following a surprisingly plain trail, had crossed over onto Catclaw range to the north half a dozen miles. And there, in the big meadow, they had discovered the strays, peacefully sleeping or grazing.

"The Big Meadow?" Levinger repeated unbelievingly. "Are you crazy?"

"Kind of wondered the same thing ourselves," the messengers admitted. "But there they are. We headed back to report."

If the previous pattern of events had been bewildering, this was worse. The Big Meadow, as it was known, was a quarter-section of land belonging to Jeb Crowley. It lay, hidden and obscure, seldom visited, in the middle of Catclaw range.

The oddity had come about when Crowley, a newcomer to the country, had discovered the hidden meadow and homesteaded it. In due time he had received title.

Since then, it had remained deep inside Catclaw, and because he and Rusty Donovan were friends, there had been no problem. Some years, Moon Star drove a herd up to the meadow and grazed it for a few weeks. Other seasons it went untouched, or else Donovan turned some of his stock in to fatten.

Having been appraised of the find, the entire crew were gathered, waiting, expectant. Everyone professed ignorance as to how the herd could have drifted to the distant pasture. Yet it could not have happened by chance; clearly they had been rounded up and driven there.

Levinger's anger blazed at sight of another crew jogging along lazily. Even in the gathering gloom of evening it was easy to see that every man was heavily armed. Here, Levinger knew, must be the riddle's answer.

Spurring, he intercepted McQuillan, who pulled up readily, the other eleven at his heels.

"I'll have a word with you," Levinger said angrily.

Again McQuillan was deceptively mild. "As many as you like," he agreed.

"Why the devil did you fellows drive off our herd?" Levinger demanded. "Stealing!"

McQuillan's eyebrows bunched like humping tomcats. "Stealing?" he repeated. "A nasty word, sir.

Especially when we were but following orders."

"And now you're lying," Levinger went on furiously. "Crowley gave no such orders!"

"You pile one insulting word atop another, but I'll be patient, since this is clearly a case of misunderstanding. You'll at least admit that Mr. Crowley hired us?"

"That much I'll grant. And I'm firing you!"

"One point at a time, if you please. We were duly hired—and paid. The cattle were moved according to orders."

"That I doubt. But why to the Big Meadow?"

"Orders." McQuillan shrugged. "After all, I was told that it is a part of Moon Star range, and you'll have seen for yourself that the cattle are there. If the boss wants it that way, isn't that his business?"

"I am known as a patient man," Levinger informed him, a statement which some of the listeners found surprising. "But there is a limit. Get off this range—and stay off!"

"Not so fast," McQuillan protested. "There is the matter of wages—"

"You say that Crowley hired you. If you think you have any money coming, look to him for it."

"We've decided that we don't care to work for Moon Star any longer, so to the devil with you and your outfit!" McQuillan retorted, and led his men toward the line.

18.

Deputy Sheriff Bob Hankinson returned without fanfare, slipping into the office adjoining the jail under cover of the settling night. He was unshaven and he looked tired, but a bed for the night was clearly not in his calculations.

"I think we should be riding," he suggested. "This time the deal is on a ruinous scale—to steal all the cattle belonging to Moon Star, including the yearlings which you recovered not many days ago."

"It runs in my mind that you had a part in that recovery," Boone reminded him, and satisfied his curiosity by asking a simple question. "You know where to go?"

"I hope so."

"Then lead the way."

They rode for some time in silence before he asked another question.

"Should we inform the Moon Star crew—or have you done so?"

"They know all about it—or think they do," was the rejoinder. "Of course, what they know and what they believe may be different matters."

Heavy darkness squeezed out the last remnants of light after midnight, clouds moving in on a high wind well overhead. At the surface it barely ruffled the few leaves still clinging to shivering limbs, but in its wail was a warning of the oncoming winter. It had been rainy and cold when Boone had returned to this country; now, following an easy interval, the arctic onslaught was to be resumed.

They snatched some sleep, then struggled awake with the aid of coffee and bacon; and were back in the saddle as the wall of night began to crack. They sighted the big meadow at the normal hour of sunrise, and there was evidence that the herd had been there. They had left a plain trail, leading north.

"I rather expected that they'd be gone," Hankinson admitted. "I *was* surprised when I found the herd here, left out in the open for a couple of days. Flaunted, you might say."

Boone studied the emptiness, frowning. Clouds and wind had kept away the frost, but the raw dankness bit into naked willows. He nodded in growing comprehension.

"This piece of land belongs to Moon Star, even though it's right in the middle of Catclaw range. I've long had the feeling that Donovan was bitterly resentful of that. Once he suggested to Crowley that Jeb should give it to him as a Christmas present. They both laughed—but the sound of a rattlesnake has something of the same quality. Am I right in guessing that Crowley's new gun crew ran the herd up here while the regulars were spending the night in town?"

"That's probably when it happened," Bob agreed apologetically. "I wasn't around to see. I'd followed a false lead—which I'm afraid was planted for me to find."

"There have been a flock of false leads flying in our faces." Boone nodded grimly. "This one, moving the herd here and leaving it to be found, still on Moon Star land, driven by a Moon Star crew—that smacks of genius."

"I agree. It has thrown dust in all our eyes. Now the bunch is being pushed toward the border—and if we catch them this time, it will be a close thing."

"And a leaden hailstorm in our faces, if we should overtake them short of Canada!"

"There'll be that, sure."

"As a deputy," Boone commended him, "you are in a class by yourself. But it runs in my mind that the job must fit your inclinations, to begin with?"

Bob grinned tiredly.

"Right you are, Boone. If you'll allow a play on your name, the chance has been a boon to me. And you've been more patient and trusting with me than I had any right to expect. Several times I've thought of telling you what it was all about, from my point of view, only I didn't like to bother you with a lot of suspicions and guesswork, which might be wrong. Part of it was my private affair. Rather than mislead you, I kept still. But the way you've trusted and backed me, under the circumstances—I owe you a lot."

"That works both ways. I take it that you see some light ahead, at last?"

"It may not be exactly a sunrise, but at least there's a dawn. I found it hard to believe at first, and I still can't entirely swallow it, but I'm sure that by now you've guessed the same—that Rusty Donovan isn't quite the disinterested friend to Jeb Crowley that he pretends?"

"The notion has occurred to me."

"Donovan's clever, and he has an astonishing amount of patience. Jeb is just the opposite, forthright in everything he does. I'm sure it never occurred to him that someone could dissemble and play a part the way Donovan has done for years. Because Jeb wouldn't do such a thing himself, it has never occurred to him that his best friend could or would treat him so."

"That jibes with my thinking—that Donovan has never forgiven Jeb for taking his girl away from him."

"That's where the trouble began—though actually, as I know, she never liked Donovan. It was always Crowley. As soon as they were married, Donovan set out to break it up, to cause trouble between them."

"I've heard it said that Jeb's wife ran away with a cattle buyer."

"She didn't. The two of them took the same train East, making it seem that way."

"How do you know all this?"

Hankinson's smile was tight. "The lady in question happens to be my mother."

Boone blinked, digesting this. "Then your sister—"

"Half-sister," Bob corrected. 'Helen is not actually a Hankinson, though she's always gone under that name. Her real name is Crowley."

Boone pulled his horse to a stop. "You mean that she's Jeb's daughter?"

"Just that. It has taken us quite a while to dig out all the facts, to fit all the pieces together, but the pattern is rounding into shape. Donovan never forgave either his friend or the girl he had wanted for marrying each other, though he pretended to. He started planning right from the start to get what he figured would be a fiting revenge on both of them. The longer it took, and the more complete the ruin for both of them, especially Crowley—well, I guess he figured that he'd enjoy it just that much more."

"He's that sort."

"I doubt if you still guess the half of it. He was the one who imported Peobody to work the whole thing—the cattle buyer—"

"Peabody!"

"The same. Donovan succeeded in making Crowley believe that his wife was in love with Peabody. Then, one day, while Crowley was away, his wife got word that her mother was very sick, perhaps dying. Her mother was two thousand miles away, on the Eastern seaboard. Evidently the letter was convincing, and my mother saw no reason to doubt it. She felt that she had to go to her mother at once, and did so. She left word with one of the crew, the only one around at the time, also a letter for her husband, in which she explained everything.

"She took the stage, and Peabody was clever enough to go on horseback, so that she wouldn't become suspicious. But when she finally got on the train, there he was—and it lent credence to the report that they were eloping. That was what Donovan had hired Peabody for. Donovan looked after the necessary details here, such as making sure that the letter disappeared; also the man who knew the facts. His name was Van Horne."

Boone repeated the name thoughtfully. It rang a bell, however faint.

"Now I've got it. Wasn't a Van Horne hanged for

horse stealing right about then?"

"He was. Donovan personally led a lynch party, to get rid of the only man who could have set Crowley straight on the facts."

"My mother arrived at her old home, to discover to her amazement that *her* mother was in good health, that she had not written any letter or known about one. Other developments were equally disturbing— such as the report that she had eloped with Peabody. She wrote back, of course, giving the facts, not once but several times. But she never received an answer."

"I can't quite understand that," Boone protested. "Jeb is bull-headed, but not to that extent."

"Helen and I have discovered that the answer lies in the fact that he never received any of her letters. The regular postmaster happened quite conveniently to get sick then, for several months. While he was recuperating—on Catclaw—one of Donovan's hands took over temporarily and ran the post office."

Tampering with the mails, managed in such fashion, had been safe enough, Donovan had overlooked no bets.

"Mother was terribly upset, of course, but she was not at all well; certainly not well enough to make an immediate return trip to try and explain. She hoped later to go back with her baby, and she was ready to start, with Helen, when she learned that Crowley had divorced her."

"Did he know about the baby?"

"I'm sure he didn't. Or if he did, he was made to believe that it wasn't his. Donovan had made good on the main part of his plan. If he couldn't have the woman he wanted, neither she nor Jeb should have each other."

"That's *really* vindictive."

"The word is too mild for such a man," Bob growled. "Mother sent one final appeal, which was never acknowledged. Then she gave up and married my father. She was desperately hard up at the time, having no money at all, and her own mother having suddenly died."

"And even after all that, Donovan wasn't satisfied!"

"He seems to have had a long range plan where Crowley was concerned. He also seems to have paid Peabody a salary, all these years, to keep an eye on us back there and report to him. We didn't know that Peabody was anywhere around, but you have to say one thing for Donovan—he's thorough."

Boone nodded, and waited.

"After Mother died, a few months ago, Helen and I were determined to come out this way and dig out the truth. She had never told us much, and of course there was a lot that she didn't know. What little Helen and I knew made us suspect a lot more. On the way out—we discovered that Peabody was on the same stage. We guessed then that he was there to keep an eye on us, and of course he was still keeping Donovan posted. That's the story."

"It's quite a story," Boone confessed. "I can understand now why Donovan tried to get you hanged as a cattle rustler. He'd have a double reason."

"A triple one, as I figure it. He was getting worried about how much we might be able to dig out, concerning events which he'd figured were well buried. So he wanted me out of the way, and of course he hated Mother also, for choosing Jeb instead of himself. Getting her son hanged as a cattle thief would be a nice touch."

"Those are two reasons."

"The third is that he's been trying to persuade Helen to marry him. She looks a lot as Mother did twenty years ago—and he's not overlooking the fact that she could be proved sole heir to Moon Star."

"It makes sense. He's picked this particular time finally to smash Jeb—emotionally, financially—in every way."

Boone could understand why Bob had been reticent about speaking of any of this until he could be sure of all his facts. Many other points were now understandable.

"Donovan must have butchered that calf—the one that Jeb figured had been killed by the homesteaders."

"I wouldn't put it past him. He's a strange contradiction of a man."

"Might come from leading a double existence all these years. Well, we'll have to keep on after the herd, fast. Levinger will be coming with the boys, as fast as he can, when he finds they're gone."

The trouble was that the main crew might arrive too late. But that was beyond their control. Hankinson nodded agreement.

"Shaping up for a showdown," he conceded, and looked thoughtfully at his gun.

19.

The lawmen, traveling fast, were the first to sight the herd. They topped a hill and saw the cattle ahead, a tired, bedraggled bunch, shoved relentlessly along by a crew who appeared to flee a nameless nemesis. Allowing his horse a breather, Boone studied the riders.

"From this distance, there's nobody that I recognize—but twice as many as are needed just for driving."

"Fifteen, maybe sixteen," Hankinson agreed. "A fighting crew."

"And if they aren't already at the border, it can't be very far away," Boone added. He searched for landmarks, finding none. "If we could find a way to slow them—"

Short of attack, that seemed out of the question, and with the riders spread out, it would be impossible to surprise more than a few and bring them under the gun. The problem was solved as other men hove into sight, coming up from the south. Moon Star was arriving, however belatedly.

Levinger had spared neither men nor horses, once he'd realized the trick being played on them. Should this herd be lost, it would ruin Crowley, to say nothing of putting finis to his own career. However heavy the odds, they were in a mood to fight.

Patience and planning had been Donovan's watchwords, and now these were paying off. Foreseeing the likelihood of such a situation, he had prepared in advance. Off to the west, still another group of horsemen were topping the horizon, their goal the common one of the herd.

"That'll be McQuillan and his gunnies," Bob observed. "Nothing like having the odds well stacked."

Here was the sort of irony that Donovan would savor, the hiring of a crew to work against Crowley, yet with the boss of Moon Star footing the bill. Though the last to be seen, they were closer than the others, and now they lost no time joining the rustler crew. Together, their numbers were formidable.

The first attempt to steal a herd had come close. Now Donovan was overlooking no bets.

"They outnumber us about two to one," Hankinson observed. "This ought to be interesting."

Aware now of the closeness of Moon Star's regular crew, the outlaws abandoned their efforts to keep the tired cattle moving. Since the showdown was at hand, it might as well be here as anywhere.

It required only minutes to swing and meet his former companions. Levinger's greeting was wry.

"They sure caught me napping," he confessed. "Doing it out in the open caught us off guard. . . . You any ideas, Boone?"

"Here's where we fight," Boone returned laconically.

"I knew you'd be with us. Since you're the law, you take charge. We'll back whatever you decide."

"Then we may as well get at it. They're splitting into two groups, so as to come at us from both sides. We've no choice but to stick together."

The rustlers were maintaining their original formations. Those who had been driving the cattle were withdrawing toward the west, McQuillan and his group cutting east. The maneuver would take time to execute, and Boone had no intention of allowing them to close a pincers at will. He put his horse to a gallop, swinging to intercept McQuillan; the others were grouped close alongside.

The outlaws had figured on having more time, intending to crush them between two fires. The promptness of Moon Star's response disconcerted them, for this would be man to man, even odds, before the other group could cut back. The raiders pulled indecisively to a sudden halt. McQuillan held them bunched, and a pair of shots shouted in warning. Here there would be no period of grace, no demand for surrender. The time for that was already past.

"Hold your fire," Boone urged, and held his own horse steady. This was reminiscent of a cavalry charge. But now the second group was moving fast, hoping to flank them as they closed.

Should the raiders hold firm in the face of attack, this could be bloody; numbers favored the rustlers, and they had counted on that to win. Anger spurred with Moon Star, and their very silence, as they drove ahead, was terrifying. Boone counted on the weight of fear to make the difference.

Fear of overwhelming odds had been counted on to hold them off, or to send them fleeing in panic. The sudden certainty that Moon Star would fight could prove disconcerting. All the rival guns were barking now, a raucous chorus like the excited yapping of hounds. Hesitation stuttered in the irregular quality of the volley, and none of the charging men faltered. Two or three rifles growled a sterner challenge, but Moon Star watched Boone and waited for his signal. It seemed incredible that so much powder could already have been burnt with no hits scored, but running horses were no easy target.

Like the two crews, two sets of emotion rode today. There was apprehension, heavy as lead in the stomach, offset by exhilaration, light and heady as the froth

a beer. It made a potent brew, and Boone raised
is revolver. The others matched his motion; the gun
lk was solid in its roar. He noticed blood on his
rm, but felt no pain; a rideless horse ran alongside,
ut now the ranks ahead had crumpled in a wild
out.

His gun was empty. Boone pulled up, and the others
id the same. Strong pride rose in him that he had
een and was again one of this crew. He punched out
ne empty shells and reloaded, glancing almost in-
ifferently to where the second group of raiders had
lowed indecisively.

"Let's take them," he said, and again lifted his
ager cayuse to a gallop.

Donovan, watching from a clump of trees, felt in-
redulity and then dismay. The branches were leaf-
ess now, as naked as he felt watching the disintegra-
ion of his crew. He'd known better than to use any
f his own men from Catclaw in this work, partly
ecause they were not gunmen, and in part because
Catclaw had to appear responsible before the world.

Yet that might have been a mistake. He'd entrusted
ll this to Peabody, who across the years had become
experienced in things outside the law. Peabody had
gathered a crew who lived by their guns.

The others, too, who had come down from across
he border, were wanted men, riders of the dim road.
It had not occurred to Donovan that such men, given

the advantage of numbers and surprise, could hesitate
or fail.

It had not entered into his calculations that he
should come into the open in such an enterprise, that
he might be forced to assume leadership when the
scales balanced between victory and the shadow of a
noose. He paid others to take the risks.

Peabody, watching alongside him, thought other
wise. He had insisted that Donovan be on hand for
this climactic moment, anticipating that it might
prove rough. Dismayed, even shocked by the turn of
the battle, Peabody did not hesitate to join in the
fight. Watching him, Donovan felt a grudging admira
tion. Through the years, Elisha Peabody had demon
strated his skill as a conniver, and now he was show
ing courage and leadership, where his life was a
stake.

Momentarily it seemed that his appearance and
example might turn the tide, balanced as closely as it
was. He almost succeeded in rallying the men of the
north, to lead them in a fresh assault. They steadied
momentarily, but fear was riding today, and de
moralization had sharp spurs. The others broke and
ran.

Peabody did not flee with them. Raging, he came
back to where Donovan still waited and watched.

"Blast you," he choked. "If you'd been with me
we'd have made it. You always were a coward where

ıere was any fighting to be done. Now you're com-
ıg with me. There's still a chance."

Donovan wet his lips. The temptation was strong.
cross the years he had dreamed as well as planned,
icturing himself in the role of a fighting man, rally-
ıg others in the face of defeat, the glorious leader
e knew himself to be. And this was the day, the hour
f destiny. It was now or not at all.

But men had been dying, horses had reared and
rashed in agony, and the acrid stench of powder-
moke was less than sweet. This was reality, and
arshness rode an icy wind. He shook his head,
ıen stared incredulously at the muzzle of the gun,
ıches from his nose. The eyes behind it were snarling
nd wicked.

"You're in this, the same as the rest of us,"
ʾeabody added. "It's your show! Now you'll sink or
wim along with the rest of us—for believe it or not,
ur skins are just as precious to us as yours is to you!
ʼome on, or I'll kilı you for the coward you are!"

It was humiliating, insufferable. Always he had
ıeen above such crass and ugly matters, the planner,
vho pulled the strings. But death looked along the
•lued barrel of the gun, mocked him from the eyes
•ehind it.

"You're spoiling everything, timing it wrong," he
ʾrotested, but the choice was no longer his.

Riding forward was easier than he had expected,

and for a few desperate moments it seemed tha
their example might yet snatch victory from defeat
It was only as he realized with horror that Peabody
was down, that the sheriff was riding at him, tha
terror reclaimed him. Donovan was pulling his horse
about when a bullet overtook him. Dimly he realized
that it had been fired by Peabody, rising on an elbow
in a last supreme effort, nemesis in the guise of a
friend. There was something ironic in the notion, but
he could not quite remember what it was.

20.

Once he was able to pause and take stock, Boone discovered that the blood which stained his sleeve bbed from a hole above his elbow. It had been leanly drilled, and with a bandage whipped around he arm, it did not bother him unduly.

Otherwise he had come through without a scratch. Bob Hankinson had not been so lucky. He grimaced, itting his horse but holding hard to the saddle horn with one hand.

"My right boot's full of blood," he explained. "Doubt if I could stand or walk. Sort of a hindrance, for some bullet seems to have creased me where I sit—and it's sore."

"We'll have to put you in a bed across from Jeb Crowley," Boone retorted. "Might make him feel better, since they say that misery enjoys company."

On the whole, they had been lucky. Three men were dead, two of them outlaws, one from either group. Lucas of Moon Star was the third. Most of the others had taken a wound or so, and some were serious.

But the raid had failed, and Elisha, angered beyond endurance, had forced his confederate into the open before shooting him in a last burst of rage. Peabody had died almost as he squeezed down on the trigger.

Donovan was querulous with pain and fever as he rode in a jouncing wagon toward town.

"I never really wanted any trouble," he protested. "Not actually. Why, Jeb Crowley's always been my friend—my best friend—all these years."

"And you know, I think he believes that," Bob Hankinson observed wonderingly, after being lifted from the same wagon and its bed of straw to one somewhat more comfortable. "He's played a double role for so long that one part was just about as real to him as the other."

The news had preceded them at Singing River. The doctor, summoned, had made a third quick trip across to the town and was waiting for his lengthy list of patients.

"Don't know but what I should move here," he observed. "Since you've taken over as sheriff, Boone, it's a new place—and plenty bloody. Fine for me, of course."

"There'll be little more of that," Helen assured him. She had hurried to meet them, her heart in her eyes, as much for Boone as for her brother. "The ver will sing again."

Boone accompanied Levinger to inform Crowley hat had happened. The cattleman, listening in nazement and bewilderment, shook his head. For ace, the imperious judgment was gone; doubt had ken its place.

"I'd never have believed it," he admitted, "especilly not of Donovan. He sure fooled me—hatin' that ay, but insistin' he was my best friend, always ready help when anything came up. And because I'd taken e girl he wanted, then quarreled, and made up fterward—I trusted him. Whatever he said, I figured could count on as gospel."

He sighed, staring at the ceiling.

"And to think he made me mistrust Rose the way did—treat her so—" The big fists corded. "Once I'm ut of here, and he's up and around again—"

"You won't have to worry about him any longer," oone returned gently. "He died this morning."

"Died? Rusty?" Crowley was like a collapsed balon. Again he studied the ceiling as though seeking me message invisible to the eyes of the others. That saves me killing him. . . . See that he gets a ood burial, will you, Boone? I guess he had that uch coming."

"There's something else," Boone added. This news ad been held to the last. "Your wife, Rose, left you omething—a daughter. And she's here in town, waiting to see you."

That was the part which Crowley found hardest to credit, that she should want to see him. Boone left them alone, making his way back to the office. If he were given a chance to occupy it, the tilt-back chair might prove comfortable. . . .

He'd been short of sleep, and he guessed he must have dozed. That made awakening all the better, for he opened his eyes to see Helen in the doorway, coming toward him. . . .